a RIVER on fire

(Stories of pain, passion, trust & betrayal)

JASVINDER SHARMA

Cedar books

Published by

Cedar books

An Imprint of

Pustak Mahal®, Delhi

J-3/16 , Daryaganj, New Delhi-110002

☎ 23276539, 23272783, 23272784 • *Fax:* 011-23260518

E-mail: info@pustakmahal.com • *Website:* www.pustakmahal.com

London Office

51, Severn Crescents, Slough, Berkshire, SL 38 UU, England

E-mail: pustakmahaluk@pustakmahal.com

Sales Centre

10-B, Netaji Subhash Marg, Daryaganj, New Delhi-110002

☎ 23268292, 23268293, 23279900 • *Fax:* 011-23280567

Branch Offices

Bangalore: ☎ 22234025

E-mail: pmblr@sancharnet.in • pustak@sancharnet.in

Mumbai: ☎ 22010941

E-mail: rapidex@bom5.vsnl.net.in

Patna: ☎ 3094193 • *Telefax:* 0612-2302719

E-mail: rapidexptn@rediffmail.com

Hyderabad: *Telefax:* 040-24737290

E-mail: pustakmahalhyd@yahoo.co.in

ISBN 978-81-223-1024-5

Edition : August 2008

Printed at : Param Offsetters, Okhla, New Delhi-110020

Dedication

Twenty-four years back, I and my sweetheart, Neelu, resolved to live under one roof. We have been through thick and thin since long and yet it seems as if we had started our journey together only yesterday. We are blessed with two tall, promising and handsome sons, Abhishek and Abhinav, both engineers. Through all these years, I have been telling my wife enchanting tales and she has been giving me a patient hearing. My first book of short stories came out in Urdu, a decade ago. Neither she nor I could read it, since we could not learn this language. Then I wrote ten successful books in Hindi, winning many awards at national level.

This, my first book in English, is dedicated to you, Neelu, my wife.

Contents

Preface **5**
1. The Rendezvous **7**
2. Scorching Days, Frosty Nights **12**
3. The Surrender **19**
4. A Wild Send-Off **29**
5. Death in the City **39**
6. The Right Compensation **44**
7. The Return of Uncle Sam **50**
8. Walking Down the Nostalgia Lane **55**
9. The Unending War **63**
10. Now or Never **69**
11. Tambola Tricks **80**
12. If Winters Come **87**
13. Breaking Away **93**
14. A Happy Ending **101**
15. Point Blank **106**
16. Second Innings **114**
17. A Perfect Butcher **120**
18. Bohemian **125**
19. Where Rainbows End **131**
20. A River on Fire **139**
21. The Beginning of an End **145**
22. Never Say Tomorrow **164**
23. A Suitable Bride **172**
24. A Dog in Manger **180**
25. Picking up **185**

Preface

First came the verse, then drama and later, in the 19th century, developed the short story, as an art form. It is undoubtedly one of the most popular and forceful forms of reading today. Its popularity stems from a variety of positive points, such as supple narrative form, artful construction and the controlled organisation around a single effect, be it exploration of a character, creation of a mood, presentation of an action, or development of theme.

The task of the writer who witnesses the disorders and injustices of society is no easier. As Thomas Mann rightly puts it, "A writer is somebody for whom writing is more difficult than it is for other people."

I am not an academic, a sociologist or a historian. I just endeavour to present a 'felt' account of areas I know something about. Chaos and anarchy all around upsets me and also motivates me to pen down a satire or a story. I see insensitive people around me and in them I wish to rekindle the anger and anguish that I feel in this imperfect and cruel world. I usually write stories on human relationships and social issues. Interpersonal relationship is the key to human psyche. In my stories, relationships are paradoxical, never simple, often confusing and disappointing.

These tales are woven around the tensions between the expectations and desires through which people define themselves and their ability to accept, or even admit the realities of the world. The world never corresponds precisely to our perceptions of it. We, humans, live under the sway of false beliefs.

In this collection, I have presented the stories of such false beliefs and mistaken identities, in which for most of the part, uncertainty and disillusionment prevail. Some of them also focus on the universal human theme of loneliness and alienation and what it does to mind. Here my responses are not reactions, but expressions of my analysed experience.

I am grateful to my publishers, especially Mr. Rohit Gupta, with whose endeavour this book came out.

My heartfelt thanks are due to my editor Ms. Neha Gupta who read and re-read my stories, giving me valuable and precious advice and suggestions to make the stories flawless and unblemished.

Now I take my seat at my computer desk, hymning lines of Robert Frost from his poem 'Road not taken' —

Two roads diverged in the wood, and I –
I took the one less travelled by,
And that has made all the difference.

— Jasvinder Sharma

The Rendezvous

Anything could have happened to me.

After my death, my people might have burnt my dead body in a pyre or buried me in the grave or might have thrown me in an oblivious foul-smelling flowing river.

Once you die, it is immaterial what happens to your mortal body. I was a Hindu of the first kind who was buried in a grave along with many other people. This had become the order of the day.

The power hungry politicians come into limelight this way and they grab power only when they incite ordinary people in the name of caste, colour, creed, language or reservations.

Many innocent lives are lost but these people can go to any limit to gratify their vote banks. For them, these killings are just cold statistics.

The bomb blast that took my life rocked the whole world but only for a few days. There were series of blasts in numerous crowded areas of different cities killing more than four thousand people.

The newspapers wrote fiery editorials as usual. The opposition roared in the Parliament. The government gave away heavy compensations to the next kin of the dead and the injured. And the situation became normal once again.

There were people of different religions, mainly Hindus and Muslims, that were killed. The blasts were so powerful that the bodies of the dead had gone beyond recognition. This became a big headache for the police and the governing authorities for some time.

Curfew was imposed and flag-march done by armed forces to drive away panic and horror for the time being from the minds of those who had escaped and were safe.

If the police kept our dead bodies for long, there was every possibility of happening a violent riot and communal clash. Our dead bodies were disposed off immediately and the situation was brought under control.

I was born Hindu but thinking me to be a Muslim I was buried hastily along other Muslims in a desperate and forlorn graveyard.

When I was alive, I dreaded to die. Whenever I attended the funeral of any known person, I became sad and gloomy for weeks not because of grief for the dead man but thinking about my own self that if I had to go from this world all of a sudden, what would happen to the fortune amassed by me through corrupt means.

The most distressing thought was that I had spent a lot of money in constructing a huge villa and a secret magnificent bar in the underground cell where I enjoyed cocktail parties and weird sexual orgies with my gorgeous female friends.

Now in reality, I was a dead man and I found myself in profound peace and tranquillity. It was such an enjoyable and eternal sleep that I was not at all ready to be alive again.

To live peacefully in this present world of million cares and tensions was such a great challenge in itself.

My dead body was lowered in the grave. Mud and sand was thrown to cover me. I felt suffocated for a while.

Then a sudden thought came to my mind. I was dead already and could not feel anything, then what was the problem now?

I had now reached a stage where there was no disagreement or conflict, where there was no concern or worry, where there was no ambition or yearning any more. There was absolute serenity and calmness all around, just living (or rather dying) without any feeling.

I was happy in my heart that no one would disturb me now. When I was alive no one let me live in peace.

I had a long list of relatives and friends, and my wife's family was also quite large. Sharing the moments of happiness and sorrows of such a large brigade of known people, my hair turned grey in the prime of my youth.

But now I was free from all those troubles. The solitary and dark 6×6 grave had become my exclusive property now.

With great ease and delight, my mortal ingredients like flesh and bones were merging with soil. I was dissolving, disappearing, vanishing, fading away and was slowly becoming extinct.

There was no haste, no urgency, no hurry and no worry on the earth for me to bother. I had lost complete concern, awareness and realisation of time, space, direction and place.

I was happy with my present state, but not much time passed when this feeling of peaceful solitude was snatched away from me.

On one doomed night, I heard the pounding sounds of digging right above my head. Look at the high-handedness of this ruthless, harsh and merciless world that it doesn't let even a dead person live in his grave peacefully.

A new dead person was lowered into the right side in my small grave just beside me.

For a few days, I lay there silent in anger and fear. To whom I could have complained?

Then I could not control myself. I asked the dead man lying on my right side, "Hello, which place you belonged to before your death?"

My new neighbour replied sadly, "It is of no importance now. It is the final place now, where I will dissolve in the earth."

My mood was spoiled. I damned him. This foolish man was despondent and unhappy even after his death. When you die you are liberated from every feeling, good or bad, pain or exaltation. No grudge or malice is left.

When my dead neighbour finished his distasteful sentence he clutched his mouth clumsily. I was enraged. When this stupid fellow doesn't want to make friends with me then why should I care much for him?

Many years rolled by. We remained dead silent.

The silence between us became so profound that one day I asked him, "Well, after all, how the hell you died, any illness?"

That man remarked as if in great pain, "In the riots of 1984, I was employed to throw bombs on public, and then in 1995 I was hit by a policeman's bullet. For years I was kept in a mortuary since no one came forward to claim my dead body. Now the mortuary was also full with unclaimed corpses of riot victims. And then in the gloomy darkness of one dismal night, they threw me unceremoniously here in your grave. You don't know how famous and dreadful terrorist I was. I was the mastermind in the serial bomb blasts that claimed more than four thousands deaths."

Saying this he started laughing boisterously like Satan.

I murmured, "My killer lies buried along with me in the same grave. It is a pity I am talking to him in a friendly way. I am afraid the end of this world has come."

Scorching Days, Frosty Nights

(Tales of nightmares from a childhood diary)

*

The same trouble surfaced in the English period today. The teacher forgot to bring his stick which was meant for giving us physical punishment daily.

Whenever it happens, we are scared even more. Our hands, buttocks and legs have a good equation with that stick. When the stick is not there, the teacher becomes more devilish.

He sent Deepak, the class monitor, to the adjoining field to pluck a wooden stick of sesame tree. All of us know that when the teacher beats us with this raw, uneven and bumpy stick, it becomes intolerable. Painful rashes on the skin appear; deep and aching bruises emerge and sometimes bleeding starts.

Filled with fear, I forgot whatever I had learnt at my home. The rough and irregular wooden stick took life out of me. I wished I could run so far where no school existed. My tender palms, little hands, buttocks, legs, all were severely injured as if my skin was peeled off.

I have to conceal all this from my mother. Whenever she looks at these excesses on my innocent and delicate body, she becomes sad and gloomy.

She starts calling the teacher names and sometimes reprimands me too. My father gets no leave from the fields. He toils there from early sunrise till twilight. He doesn't bother about my studies. He just wants me to grow up quickly so that he can teach me how to handle the plough effectively.

Mother is a bit sensitive. Whenever she sees the scars of severe beating on my body, on that day, she doesn't let me do the domestic jobs like cutting fodder or tending the cattle. She says, "My dear son, you pay attention to your studies and get liberated from this mean ancestral job of agriculture."

*

Today it was a day of total relief and fun. Till afternoon, we were free.

Before recess, we had the periods of drawing and art & craft. The Hindi ma'am was on leave. We were playing freely in the classroom.

The noise level of our class rose so high that it reached the Headmaster's room. No one among us could make out anything when the Headmaster made a sudden attack on us with his thick stick.

It was like a brutal lathi-charge by the angry police on uncontrollable rioters.

The headmaster caned us mercilessly. Someone's head broke, while another's leg was hit hard.

I hid immediately under the table.

He saw me and dragged me out and gave me an exemplary thrash.

The class was dead silent as if curfew was imposed.

The headmaster left us as a winning army leaves behind the dead and injured defeated enemy. A few moments after that, we were the same again.

Once again the same old *masti ki pathshala*!

*

Today the English teacher took two continuous periods. He taught us that tenses were of twelve kinds. The Hindi ma'am had taught last week that tenses were of three kinds – present, past and future.

Suddenly it occurred to me and I stood up and asked the teacher about this anomaly.

The teacher didn't relish it. He picked up his stick and took me to task for this dare. I could not understand my fault.

Later, I asked my friend where I was wrong. He warned me never to challenge a teacher's wisdom. He explained that the teacher was right. In English, there are twelve tenses like Present Indefinite Tense, Present Continuous Tense.... I realised how stupid I was!

So baffling this English language is! We dare not ask the teacher. We are stuck at the present tense for the last two months. We repeatedly forget the identity of sentences as to which tense they belong and then what are the forms of verbs to be used, and the helping verbs etc. There is a lot of confusion. Only one or two students follow that humbug.

We apply the regular method and mug up numerous sentences from Hindi to English but when the teacher asks something different, we are caught in his net. The English grammar is very complicated. Rules changes at every step and there are thousands of exceptions.

The teacher gave us a small test of translating into English; like He goes to school, I go to market, Sita sings a song, The washerman washes clothes, etc.

Then everyone's notebook was checked.

Mohan sits with an intelligent boy. He cleverly copies down from him and never gets punishment. I sit with Radha who herself is very poor in English. So I get a beating daily.

*

Today the teacher was probably not feeling well. He didn't beat us with his cruel stick.

He ordered the students to bend down and catch their ears, bringing hands from behind, a posture like a chicken. We remained in that pose for minutes together.

All the blood had gathered on our faces and ears. The legs were badly tired and had started aching. The body had started shivering. Eyes were fainting.

Whenever we tried to straighten ourselves a bit, stealing eye of the teacher, the teacher would notice us and rebuke in a very filthy language. Thank god the bell rang!

When the teacher left, he kicked the buttocks of Sohan who fell on his face. He scolded him calling bad names to his mother and sister. He cursed him, calling him foolish, idiot and stupid countryman.

We don't hate him much when the teacher rebukes us. But when he attacks us with his brutal stick or kicks us with his heavy boots, he looks like a cruel devil.

God knows, when these teachers will die of a heart attack!

*

In the morning assembly, the headmaster gave a strange lecture to us. He advised us to remain far from cigarette, wine and bad company. These teachers themselves smoke in front of us and after the school break, and take to drinking in the school itself.

I did not listen to what he said. I kept on whispering to Mohan.

Today the first period was of Social Studies and the teacher was on Census duty. The Headmaster Sir took the class.

He started teaching us English. He asked me to stand up. Possibly he had noticed me talking during his assembly lecture.

My whole body started shuddering. The headmaster ordered, "Come near the blackboard and write — sweep, sleep, speak, walk, talk, write…."

I knew the dangerous plot behind all this humbug. I was sure that all my spellings would be wrong. He was looking for the excuses to flog me. And then the teacher took his rod and took his full revenge. He looked like my father who whips his pigheaded and obstinate bullocks.

"People were right to imagine that I never experienced any financial difficulty. I travelled widely, befriended many women and I really had a true taste of a colourful life.

"But gentlemen! I want to share this with you for the first time that I have lived a life full of paradoxes. I never did anything which could give me some comfort or solace. Everyone jilted with me at my bizarre anecdotes but no one took me seriously.

"Everybody thought me an extrovert and a laughable character and came to me in search of tomfoolery and pranks. I told them some hilarious jokes and funny things which were false and half-truths. These were just make-beliefs and hearing them they were delighted.

"You know a joke is a very serious thing. I cracked pieces of pranks and gags on my personal life just to please my listeners. Whenever I tried telling them something sombre about myself they laughed over that, thinking it to be a part of my comic material. My image as the happiest and a jolly good fellow created much troubles for me in my real life.

"I too am human, subject to humiliations and depressions but my friends never thought that way. If I told them any truth about life or about my dejection or frustration, they didn't accept it and that left me unhappy so often. To whom I should unfold my heartfelt secrets remained a hitch for me.

"Anyhow, I suffered many setbacks due to this. Womenfolk never took a serious interest in me. Many old women were my fans but younger ones shunned me.

"In my college days, I had a yearning to befriend older-than-me ladies whom we friends addressed as sexy aunties.

I fell down and then he smacked me with his robust leather shoes. I was not a football which would shoo away when knocked severely. Does the Government hire these teachers only to beat the students?

I hear our parents talking to each other. They become happy most of the time thinking that the teachers are very strict and control the class effectively through rod.

Only once, a complaint came against a teacher. Sohan was given a hard blow on his ears and his mother came to the Headmaster.

Gopal's father was also present there. Before the Headmaster could justify his staff's brutality, Gopal's father requested the Headmaster with folded hands, "How hard you may beat my son, I won't complain but make him study well. After all, he has to face the Board Examinations this year."

*

There was no electricity in the village the whole night.

In the evening, mother had kept me busy in petty household errands and odd jobs of the fields. At night, I thought of completing the homework in the light of candle but I was so tired that soon my eyes closed.

In my dreams, my condition was miserable. All my teachers thrashed and flogged me.

When I woke up in the morning, my body was soaked in sweat due to panic and terror. With trembling feet, I entered the school. I was sure all the teachers would tear off my skin today as I had not done my homework of any subject.

But there was an atmosphere of great relief and jubilation in the school today.

It was the Teacher's Day. All the periods were free. The students were making merry. I completed my pending homework, otherwise I was to be taken to task tomorrow.

The Surrender

Things had gone from bad to worse.

It seemed evident to Seema now that either she would have to say sorry to her students or be prepared to quit the college.

The way she was being grilled emotionally, it was becoming clear that she would have to bow before the student community.

Media was exposing her everywhere depicting her as an arrogant and proud woman.

Seema being the head of physical education department of the Government Girls College commanded a senior position in the college.

For the first time she was annoyed and lost her cool. During the rehearsal of a sports event, she slapped a student in front of the whole class. Though the student was at fault, but a teacher is expected to restrain her temper these days.

Time has changed now. Those days are the thing of past when a teacher took the liberty to scold or snub the pupil.

Media had exaggerated and highlighted a minor issue to this extent. On the very first day, the students released a press statement that they would boycott classes till Seema didn't tender an apology.

In the evening, Seema received a call from a local journalist. He demanded twenty thousand rupees from her to tilt the whole matter in her favour. Seema rebuked him and the very next morning the whole group of city's media persons had raised an alarm against her. They had dug up Seema's past life also.

God knows who was giving them these bits of information of her gloomy past. She had now forgotten about her horrible past with much effort. And once more she was being brought before that horrible chain of events of her youthful days.

All the girls of the college had turned against Seema. They had boycotted their classes. Gate meetings were held daily, slogans were raised and even effigies of Seema along with that of College Principal were burnt. The newspapers published sensational and lead stories. All the television channels were covering the day-to-day developments.

An atmosphere of tension and mistrust was created to malign Seema. The girls were becoming violent day by day now. They had issued an ultimatum that if Seema madam would not appear before them within three days to say sorry, they would go on an indefinite hunger strike demanding her dismissal from the college.

Seema had imprisoned herself in her flat in the staff colony. Her colleagues were keeping her informed about the moves of the students.

The Principal madam visited her daily. In the first week, she had sympathy for Seema but as the events turned violent, she changed her tone. Last night she openly told Seema that in the end she would have to surrender. The Director of Education had clearly told Seema to settle the matter amicably before the last day of the ultimatum.

Seema thought about many alternatives. She thought of seeking a voluntary retirement from the service. She would get a handsome pension which would be sufficient for her. Moreover she would get royalties on her books. She had a good bank balance. Then why should she lower herself before the students?

But then, she was worried. At this point of her life where will she go? She was living there for the past twenty years with comforts and grace. She had made good friends and a good reputation. Leaving the job could create problems of a safe and secure accommodation and social circle.

Within a week of that turmoil, the college was losing its reputation. The Principal was more worried. There was a clear change in her soft attitude towards Seema. She had clearly told her that she should show greatness of heart and come forward and forgive the students so that normal life could return to the college.

Seema was in the same fix fifteen years ago when she and her husband Vivek were in direct confrontation with each other.

Then also a question of life and death had propped up. The circumstances had gone totally against her but she was not dismayed. She had resolved not to bow before her husband and his family. There were storms roaring in her heart when she fell in love with Vivek.

Their case was not exactly falling in love with each other. This was the story of the period of rising violence and soaring prices in the early seventies soon after the war of Independence of Bangladesh.

In those days, a woman's role was restricted within the four walls of her house. Very few girls entered college. They were married before passing out high school. Parents thought it unrespectable to allow girls to participate in games or take a course in physical education.

Seema was a tall and long-haired girl with attractive features. Her father was a colonel in the army. She was a fine sportswoman.

Her father wanted her to be a tennis star of international repute. But there was something else in store for her. After the sudden demise of her father in a massive heart attack, there was a great turbulence in the life of Seema and her family. There were better facilities and good coaches in Delhi but her mother had to shift to her remote native town.

One way was to keep Seema at a hostel in Delhi but in those days, a girl child was not given much importance. Seema's two younger brothers were in the undergraduate classes. With pension money, how could her mother spend to help Seema fulfil her dream to become a national sports star? Her mother asked her to use her excellence in sports to find a good job.

Seema's academic profile was superb. She readily got the job of a physical education teacher in a government college.

Then she completed her post graduation and pursued a Ph.D. She had become an authority in her field and was made the head of physical education department. Many good families were ready to take her as a bride.

In an Inter-University Youth Festival, her meeting with Vivek came as a turning point in the lives of both of them. He fell in love with her at the first sight.

He had recently cleared his civil services training and was posted as an Assistant Collector. He was the chief guest at the youth festival which lasted for a week and that was enough time for him to come closer to Seema.

Seema had not taken these meetings with Vivek too seriously. She was an academic type of woman. Vivek was handsome, lively, vibrant and good-humoured. He had resolved in his mind that Seema was made for him only. Though he did not disclose his mind before her but he assumed that she too liked him. He decided to marry her.

Seema's mother had no objection to the marriage proposal sent by Vivek. She wanted her daughter to get married now.

Vivek sent his subordinate officer secretly to Seema's house to enquire from her mother if they were interested in marriage.

When Seema learnt this from her mother, she didn't relish this. Her mom said in satire that her boyfriend had sent the proposal. Seema had no inkling about such serious development. She thought that Vivek should better have sought her intension before sending a proposal of marriage directly to her mother.

Next day, she reached his office. She said in an angry tone, "Sir, we are not living in the 16th century where the matters regarding love or marriage were kept secret even from the bride. If you had something to say, you should have told me. You should not use your rank or office to pressurise my mother."

Vivek was flabbergasted. He was a self-made man, a sincere person not well-versed in the art of wooing women.

He said hesitantly, "Well, Miss Seema, please don't get me wrong. I started liking you from the day one but I couldn't dare to disclose my true feelings to you. I admit I should have told you about my inner feelings before sending my officer with a marriage proposal to your mom. Now when a process of weaving a lifelong relationship with you has been initiated, please let me know how we should begin."

Seema's temper was still running very high. Ignoring all the good moments spent with Vivek in the past, she went on, "Sir, how strange it is that in two or three meetings with me in a function, you decided on your own that you would marry me. Who gave you the right to give my mother an impression that I knew all about this love game and I sent you to feel her pulse? I am full of remorse as to why I was so friendly and kind with you during that fest."

Vivek took a more defensive position, "Look Seema, try to understand me. You are not respecting my genuine feelings for you. There was no ill-will in my heart. Due to reservations and paucity of time I could not tell you my heartfelt emotions. I sent the proposal in the fear that I may not lose you. Don't get me wrong."

Seema was still filled with wrath, "Being an IAS officer, you were dead sure that when you will send a marriage proposal, any damn girl and her family will come running after you with folded hands. You don't know that my father was a Senior Defence Officer and I am myself holding a Class One post for the past five years. My salary is more than yours."

Vivek said, "Okay, let me admit that I made a mistake but there should be some solution to this mess. Please calm down. I am really sorry to hurt your feelings. Let us leave all that bitter talk for the moment. What will you take, coffee or tea?"

He pressed the bell. Seema was in a bad mood. She said 'No thanks' and rushed out of Vivek's office.

There was no further conversation between them for three years. Vivek was promoted as District Collector and was posted in some other city. Seema had forgotten all about that. She was busy in writing textbooks and features for the journals of international repute. She had name and fame. Her mother showed her some good marriage proposals but she couldn't say her final yes anywhere.

Once again she encountered Vivek. In a marriage, she had gone to Delhi. Vivek was also there. He was still unmarried. Seema's uncle initiated talks with Vivek's father about a possible matrimonial alliance of Vivek with Seema. When Seema's mother asked her, she couldn't say no.

There was no problem in the first year of their marriage. Seema stayed at her in-laws' house. The problem began when she started getting phone calls from her college. She had been on leave for three months. The syllabus of her students was incomplete. In a subdued tone, Vivek proposed her to leave the job.

Seema reasoned out that being the Head of the Department, she had many responsibilities to handle. She had not even dreamt of leaving her job. However they had never discussed anything about this before marriage.

She said frankly, "Look Vivek, the time has changed now. For today's woman, to be self-sufficient is very essential. With great toil, I have secured an honourable position for myself in the society. Sports is not just a career for me. It is like a passion. I won't leave my job at any cost."

Vivek could not argue much. Seema joined her duties. Vivek was in a Ministry at Delhi. There was a distance of five hundred miles between them but they didn't feel it because they pined for each other.

Sometimes he went to her and sometimes she came to Delhi and stayed for a week. Seema's leave account had become nil. Vivek too had a hectic routine. But they still loved each other and were in touch.

They were very much familiar with the mentality of their older generation. No one could disrupt their romantic married life in the first three years. Then the bitter and trying time came.

Vivek was pressing hard that Seema should leave her job and stay with him so that they could think about having a baby and a settled life. The differences between them were increasing. And then came a turn in their life when both started shunning each other. There was no fight or abuse or no levelling of any charges on one another. Both were bent upon suppressing each other.

Vivek gave a final ultimatum to her to leave the job. She didn't respond for a month. Next month, he didn't pay her a visit. Then the deadlock started.

Seema's mom died in a car accident and Vivek didn't come. The ditch of suspicion and indifference between them was getting deeper and deeper.

She stopped waiting for him any more. She devoted herself totally to her subject. She was a number one author on sports now.

Now after this recent row in the college, media had started bringing the tormented tale of suffering and agony of Seema before the public. She was completely shaken.

She had thought that the ghost of bitterness between her and Vivek was buried five years ago, but media had started proving that she was an arrogant woman who had not cared for her worthy husband, so how could she feel sorry for her students now?

With change in the attitude of her Principal, Seema remained sleepless the whole night. She thought, would she be able to live calmly by living in a state of constant and perpetual war with her own self, her husband or with her students whom she loved so much? Vivek never coerced.

Seema in her arrogance did many excesses on him. She always tried to prevail upon him. He only wanted that she should leave her job and be a good mother to his children. Can she forgive him now? Can't she apologise? She was sure he would own him.

Then she thought that it would still be better if she leave her job and go back to Vivek and live with him. Then it came to her mind that she should not run away from the circumstances.

She had harmed the self-esteem of Vivek and she had also harmed the self-respect of the girl whom she had slapped in front of more than fifty students.

If Seema would say sorry to her, she would not belittle herself. She would forgive and only then she would be forgiven.

The whole night she pondered over her dilemma.

In the morning, she called the Principal madam to her house. She told her about her decision. The Principal shrieked with joy, "Thanks Seema, you saved all of us."

The Principal madam was dialling her senior officer to tell him that the crisis was resolved.

She saw Seema was on her phone talking to her husband Vivek. As she finished, her eyes were moist and full of tears.

She had understood the significance of pardon.

With enthusiastic steps, both Vivek and Seema were now rushing towards the college.

∞

A Wild Send-Off

They were a group of boisterous low-ranked government officers partying at a bar. Their average age was around fifty. Everyone was boasting loudly and exaggerating his little achievements. When they got drunk, more than two persons started talking at a time. A chaos was created all around. The scene looked like a downmarket town fish market.

And then, one of them, an old and frail officer raised his voice. He seemed to be the seniormost of them all. He had, of late, a cataract operation done. The doctors had corrected his eyesight with imported lenses. Without his usual spectacles, he was looking quite odd.

He was in perfect senses but he was trying to control his steps unnecessarily and that was a clear indication that he would gulp down still more pegs of wine, for the occasion was one of enjoyment, and wine was plenty and available for free.

The officer saying 'Hello Please' raised his voice, "Look brothers, we are talking in small groups and this is not graceful to the occasion. We have assembled here to celebrate the farewell party of Mr. Khanna who is going to retire today. I suggest that every one of us should present himself one by one so that we may relish each other's company. We will request Mr. Khanna to deliver his speech, but before that we should share with each other our individual experiences of life. We can start alphabetically or according to our age. Yes, what is the general opinion on according to age? Okay, it will be better. Yes, Mr. Prakash, you are the youngest, please share your experiences with us – some interesting anecdotes."

Mr. Prakash put off his cigarette. Clearing his throat he started his tale, "Well, I don't have much to say. You all know that I joined this office on compassionate grounds. My father died due to heart attack and out of compulsion I joined this office as a clerk at a tender age of eighteen. I had appeared in the final year of my graduation."

"My class fellows were stunned when they learnt that I had taken up the job of a petty clerk. I always dreamt of becoming an IAS officer but my papa's death made me sit on a diary-dispatch seat in this office so that our family could retain the government accommodation and with mom's pension and my salary I could get my two marriageable sisters settled.

"In the beginning, I was finding my job a mismatch to my ambition. Sometimes after the office hours, I would walk towards my college hostel. My friends would look at me with awe and surprise. They wondered why I did all this and recommended me to leave that petty job and strive for higher goals.

"That evening was the end of the session. I met Geeta in the college library. I had left the college but my affinity with

Geeta was still intact. We were batch-fellows since our school days. We went to the café. The waiter brought coffee for us. He knew us. We used to go there quite often.

"Geeta was a bold girl. Her background was sound. I became sadder when I met her. She didn't like my taking up a petty government job.

"She pressed me to take other prospective routes for a better career. She prompted me to do a post graduation course and compete for officer level jobs but I was getting comfortable with my present job.

"I had started preparing for the promotional tests here. I had befriended many frustrated people of the office. This insignificant post of clerk and trivial matters involved me so passionately and emotionally with the atmosphere here that I started loving the office too much.

"The office took me in its fold in the same way as a fierce full-flooded seasonal river engulfs everything on its way, be it trees, bushes or tiny settlements.

"Then I married a homely girl of an office superintendent. With all those compromises, how far could I go?

"My condition was similar to that of an innocent boy who had gone to sleep after weeping for a few hours demanding a chocolate and had forgotten about the whole affair by the morning.

"I was completely absorbed in paltry official matters. In all this humbug when my high-spirited youth eluded me I didn't realise.

"Now I am nearing fifty-two. In my youth, I was always worrying about my sisters. Now at this age, I remain fretful about my sons, one of them is studying law and the other in an Engineering college.

"The place where I should have been by now, I have reached there. There is no magical turn left or any other dream destination beyond it.

"The extraordinary happiness which I was dreaming to seek right from my childhood now seems an illusion to me. It remained only a mirage for me throughout my life.

"The government has made me a petty officer but I have a deep sense of loathing in my heart. In the prime of my youth, had I listened to Geeta and had I rebelled against my social pressures, I would have been a Joint Secretary now. I was a very brilliant student. In my matriculation examination, I had secured a merit position."

Mr. Prakash's face looked pale and fatigued. He lit a cigarette. For a while, everyone had become sullen and gloomy.

Some persons were lifting glassful of wine and were swirling more and more. Now it was the turn of Mr. Verma to share his unique anecdotes. He was quite a humorous fellow.

Mr. Verma swallowed his unfinished peg of rum and raised his voice. He was a happy-go-lucky and a flirt type of person.

He was open and frank and everyone liked his bohemian style of life. He was very witty, outspoken and was always ready with a dirty joke to explode laughter in the group.

Mr. Verma narrated his tale, "Well, dear friends, my life has remained an open book before you. I have fully enjoyed my life. I belonged to a prosperous family. I got a working wife."

In fact, I was successful in one or two cases but my fun-loving and non-serious nature kept me far from good and young girls.

"And when my marriage became dull and monotonous, my interest in younger-than-me ladies grew more and more intense. My fast growing silver hair and bulging tummy kept them away from me.

"But at one point of time, I really got a remarkable crush of my life. Those days I was a training officer of our staff college. A sweet young girl in a batch was fascinated by my effusive and vociferous verbosity and witty talks.

"She was slightly dark and bulky. That was the reason I was not much fascinated by her looks. We Indians fall badly for fair colour. Now I reflect that I should not have broken her heart.

"Well, her name was Vijaya. After the training class, she came to meet me in my section. She was a young girl in her early twenties. I was forty plus then. I wasn't so mature but my hair had started turning grey near my ears.

"When she came to meet me in my section, all the colleagues in the section were wonderstruck. I offered her a seat and ordered a tea for her.

"There was a gap of many years between us. She was mounting towards mature years while I was sliding towards midlife.

"She was in a humorous mood that day. Seeing my name plate she remarked, "Your name sounds girlish, isn't it?"

"I blushed and could not think of anything else but to reply, "And your name is too masculine." Glancing at me with cute eyes, she laughed loudly.

"For the first time I felt hesitation in front of my subordinates not because she was of opposite sex but because she was much younger to me.

"Before that incident, I had never cared what other people thought of my wayward behaviour and naughty relations with women in my office.

"I knew that people considered me a big womaniser who enjoyed more in the company of women. The women sitting with me were totally blatant, open and frank. They were normally older and completely frigid and insensitive.

"They were there to listen to my verbal nonsense and cheap jokes and titbits. I could say any nasty thing to them. I could take their hand in my hand, could kiss them invariably and enjoy the intimacy of some of them in bed also.

"The most irritating thing that my jolly good frigid ladies experienced was when Vijaya came to meet me the second time and that too within a week.

"I was very happy but in heart of heart I was also getting fearful. It was the only mistake of Vijaya that when she met me I had eaten much of my youthful life.

"I was fast racing towards fifty and she had just crossed twenty. She made an exciting conversation. I was seeing clearly that this girl had developed an infatuation for me.

"To get into a serious relationship with a girl of much lower age was my long cherished dream and now I was happy that it was going to come true.

"But I was both scared and withdrawn. I was frightened. I was afraid imagining all the time lest something wrong might not happen and what all the people would say. It was a clear case of calf love. My old women taunted me sarcastically. They started calling me uncle.

"Vijaya was not that beautiful but she had a fashionably plump, supple and sexy body. She had big eyes. She was quite bold and daring.

"She had a good interest in literature. I had also graduated with English Honours, so we exchanged many good ideas and discussed books written by Bacon, Thomas Hardy and Tolstoy.

"For hours we used to discuss literature. With her my condition had become similar to that of a naïve kid foolish enough to pick up a burning coal with his bare hands.

"She had brought a squall and a violent tempest in my straightforward and unruffled life. I was flying high in air.

"She was as crazy as a fast virgin small river which has a scurry to flow down very swiftly. I was a bit like calm and collected pool of water. I had seen much of passions of love and lust in my life.

"Due to this restraint and hesitation I did never propose to go out on a date with her. She implored many times, "Sir, let us sneak for an outing to a nearby hill station, say Simla or Manali. We will have a great fun. What if we had to stay there for a night or so?"

"I found an excuse every time. I was scared of the society. With ladies of my age I was quite secure. Their husbands knew all about these cold affairs and they were not threatened, but going out with a young lady was becoming a challenge for me.

"I would change my decisions daily since the stakes were very high.

"And, one day I went out with her in the city itself. We strolled in the auto-rickshaw in the whole town but I could not find a single place where I could feel secure or at ease with her.

"A passionate thought came to my mind. I decided to take her to a hotel and have sex with her. She too would not have resisted. But thinking her to be a pretty young girl I could not dare to propose such a frightful resolution.

"I wanted to take her to a secluded place. Everywhere I found familiar faces. She was chirping and was proposing many different alternatives like going to a movie or for boating in the lake. At last we went to café in the university.

"Walking with her I had this feeling that I had gone into my teenage and had become much younger than my real age.

"Then comparing our ages, I was filled with a sense of guilty that I was committing a blunder. Why is a real love not possible without a sense of guilt and remorse?

"I was petrified and scared of the outcome of this unmatched love. I was afraid of the people around me, of the society and even afraid and uncertain of my own self.

"I sincerely wanted to get entangled with her but not so deeply. I wanted to touch and feel her softly, but not sway in the strong and gripping passions and painful pangs of love.

"Vijaya was damn crazy to have me and my company, and once she unfolded her inner feelings that she would never desert me. She was getting possessive of me to the extent that we had started going to café daily.

"We used to sit there for hours unmindful of known people around. A few friends of mine advised me on my involvement with a girl half my age but we were unmoved.

"Then the moment of final test came at last. We made a plan to spend a night somewhere out of city. At the last moment I changed my decision.

"At the appointed hour I kept sitting at my house. She rang many times from the station but I switched off the mobile. When I went to the office after a week I was a changed man.

"I called back all those old flame ladies and made myself busy cracking light jokes to them. Vijaya came but I made excuses that the boss could call me anytime. I avoided her, deserted her, and offended her.

"When she came again I surrounded myself with old frosty ladies which were safe and secured for me. I distanced myself from her. I shut myself encased in the same manner as wise housewives keep pickles in airtight jars.

"Now at this age when I remember those wonderful years when I really loved someone from the inner core of my heart I become sad and gloomy. I reflect that I intentionally cheated the only girl I really loved in my life."

The listeners had become sad and gloomy. There was a distressing silence all around. After that many other people narrated their unique, heartbreaking and mind swaying tales but there was no magic or charm in them.

They were all justifying their failures and inefficiencies. All these people had wasted their youthful days in inconsequential and petty pursuits.

They were now remorseful, feeling dejected, sad and spent up. And when they became busy in trivial official politics, they started talking in small groups again.

ꝏ

Death in the City

The telephone rang in the early hours of morning and the whole house was distressed by the fear of something unfortunate happening.

A few minutes later, Parvati while giving bed tea to her two sons said in a sad tone, "Janki *Tai* has passed away. Chander had made a call early morning. The funeral is at 4 o' clock in the afternoon today."

Everyone in their family was an office-goer except Parvati. Everyone was depressed. No one was moved by the death. How this humbug will be settled was their main concern. No one was willing to take a sudden leave from office.

The elder son kept the tea cup on the settee and stretched his legs. After the death of his father in a sudden heart attack, the elder son had to struggle for the post of head of the family, his widowed mother Parvati being his sole rival.

The younger son of Parvati was a little bit of jovial nature. He took least interest in the petty household affairs. He was newly married and always remained busy with his bride.

Yawning and stretching himself indolently, the younger son asked in inquisitiveness, "How did the grandaunt died? I mean she was quite hale and hearty when we last visited them."

Sitting on sofa, Parvati said, "Chander told that it was a natural death. Chander's father gets up early in the morning. As usual today when he arose to set out for the temple he observed that Janki *Tai* was sleeping without making any noise. He became suspicious as she was in a habit of snoring. Chander's father shook her and felt her pulse. It was all calm and quite. *Tai* must have gone to the heavenly abode in the late midnight. God grants such lucky deaths only to His blessed few."

The elder son had an unusual habit of finding fault in everything said to him. Right from his birth, it was his nature to doubt even plain things.

This habit was also due to the nature of duties he performed at his office. He was in government audit department and it was his routine work to raise objections on bills, files, contracts and other records. That was the main reason of his eccentric habit. His in-laws, friends and all other known people never came his way and avoided any worthless arguments with him. Hearing about the reason of Janki *Tai's* death, he said, "How is it possible?"

Usually he confused everyone with this uncanny sentence. Reacting to his objection, the opponent would start justifying himself giving reasons and facts but by that time this weird man would have raised another objection.

He raised his first objection, "How is this possible that a person may die in his sleep? They have a joint family. She might have died of a massive heart attack or brain haemorrhage."

He would have continued his verbal bombast but he was stopped by an intervention. The newspaper hawker rang the doorbell. He handed the monthly newspaper bill and Parvati got up to pay him.

It was their daily routine. Parvati got up before five in the morning and prepared bed tea for herself and her sons, while they would sit in the drawing room, read newspapers and would discuss worldly affairs.

The younger one would sit for a while after tea and would again go to his bedroom to sleep for a few more minutes. Parvati and her elder son would argue for long. Parvati's both daughters-in-law avoided bed tea. They would get up around seven and start getting ready for the office.

When Parvati came back after making payment of newspaper bill, the elder son commanded to his mother, "Well, I will take a half casual leave from my office today and attend the funeral at *nigambodh*. You may go there on *kiriya* ceremony a few days later."

Parvati was taken aback. She did not agree with the one-sided decision taken by her elder son. She was thinking differently.

She said, "No, not these ways as you say. On the funeral day, the entire kinfolk assemble. If I will not go, what my brothers-in-law, their wives and other elderly people will think of me? If you don't attend a marriage function, there is not much fuss made on that issue. You send gift or money and no one is annoyed. But a death is a serious occasion. No excuses can be made and no one listens to such lame duck excuses that leave was not granted from office. It becomes difficult to justify yourself later on. A local funeral has to be given a top priority. I must go. You decide yourself who would stay at home today."

The younger son was busy in his own thoughts. He had not felt the gravity of the death in their kinfolk.

The elder son proposed a new formula, "Pankaj, you take leave today and in the afternoon take mom to Shakti Nagar before the start of funeral journey, while I'll stay at home."

The younger son cried defensively, "I am sorry, I can't take leave today. It is stocktaking day in my office and on Monday the inspection team is coming to check our records, so I can't apply for leave in any way." He got up and headed towards his bedroom and went for a short nap.

Both daughters-in-law of Parvati appeared in the drawing room. They openly showed their inability to take an unexpected leave from office.

Now it was Parvati and her elder son's accountability to solve the problem of attending funeral. Her elder son wanted to go there alone but she didn't approve of it. Her anger knew no bounds.

It was her daily duty to guard the house. The kids came back from their schools at 2 in the afternoon. The dusting and cleaning jobs were done by 11 in the morning by the maid-servants.

Parvati's sons and their wives left for their office by 8 in the morning. Attending to her grandchildren, giving them meals, seeing that they complete homework etc were Parvati's responsibilities. Theirs being a joint family the finance of the whole house was controlled and regulated by Parvati herself.

Today for the first time her fury shot up. She was not as much perturbed and moved by the death of Janki *Tai* as much was she horrified to see the self-centred and mean behaviours of her sons and their selfish wives.

They were not ready to take a day's leave for her sake. By taking working girls for her sons, she had invited this trouble herself and was now in deep water.

Everyone refused to relieve her. She went mad with resentment and at last burst out, "For how long will I take care of your responsibilities? I am 75 now. I may leave this world any day. Who will come to your house to bereave and console you? You will have to hire labourers to take my corpse to the *Nigambodh* pyre. Now I knew the reason why you always stop me from visiting my relatives. You use me as a maid servant so that your kids get fresh food and the doors of your house remain open all the day. You are all selfish, crooked, downmarket and self-seeking. You can't spare a day for me. You don't realise that the woman who died today was real aunt of your father."

Parvati's tears rolled over her cheeks. Hearing this hue and cry, the younger son came out from his bedroom and sensed the whole dilemma. He was a man with a lively nature having a good sense of humour.

He drew attention of everyone and proposed, "Well, mom, don't cry. Let us do one thing. Big brother is ready to take a leave to take you to the funeral. Now let the rest three of us write slips of our names and hold a draw. The person whose name would come would have to stay at home today."

A cruel and nasty smile flashed on everybody's face.

The Right Compensation

Sharad was awfully upset that day. It came like a bolt from the blue. His closest friend Harnam died this morning.

Sharad was in the cremation ground. Harnam's dead body lay there. He died of a massive heart attack. Sharad was not that much upset by the death of his friend. Another anxiety was upsetting him.

He had lent two lakh rupees to Harnam, secretly from his credit card and no one knew about it, not even his wife. Harnam had also kept the matter secret from his family. That was the reason Sharad was totally upset today. There was no chance of return of his money.

How could he tell Harnam's wife, who was weeping so heartrendingly? Hell had fallen on her. She had to look after her two school-going kids. In no way, she was in a position to return the loan given by Sharad.

Harnam had requested Sharad to help him and Sharad was taken by his promise. Harnam had said that he was in a deep debt trap. In a few months, his financial position would improve. The pending bills would be cleared and the cash flow would increase. He requested Sharad to lend him two lakh rupees. Sharad had faith in him and keeping it a secret between the two friends, he gave him the money.

Before coming into business, Sharad was a government employee. He was content with his job but his wife was not satisfied with it. She belonged to an affluent family. Her brother was a captain in the merchant navy and his monthly tax free income was more than three lakhs.

Sharad was taken by the laudatory plans of his wife. He took premature retirement. He got ten lakh rupees from the office. A sum of five lakhs was given to him by his brother-in-law as a soft interest free loan, saying that he won't demand it back himself, if Sharad progressed in life, he might at his will return it.

Sharad had a good experience in the field of publication of books. He was an employee of the State Academy of Art, Culture and Languages. This office published books and periodicals worth crores of rupees every year.

Sharad's colleagues were masters of their game. They got kickbacks in allotment of books to authors and made thousands in the purchase of paper. Sharad was a novice in this game. It was not in his blood to hook a contractor to bribe him. He was tactless and a sentimental fool.

His wife called him an inexperienced man. Then to make the matter worse, Sharad became the executive member of the anti-corruption cell of the union. All the roads to earn easy money through unfair means were closed for him now.

In his heart, Sharad too wanted to earn money and get rich but his reputation as a straightforward and honest man was the main obstacle. It prevented the contractors to grease his palm. They feared that he might get them blacklisted.

Sharad's wife was shrewd and business-minded. He discussed everything with her. His wife taught many tricks to him to extract money from the customer's pocket in exchange for the favours made. Sharad could not perfect himself in this art.

Then at last, his wife declared that Sharad should leave the job and start some business. He got ten lakhs as retirement money and five lakhs was loaned to him by his wife's brother.

His experience and hard work helped him to rise unusually in the publication business. He made a good reputation and the fact that he was sincere and honest, he earned a steady goodwill.

In just five years, he turned his fifteen lakhs into seventy-five lakhs. He was reckoned as the most innovative publisher in the country now. He started launching books of eminent politicians and statesmen. His close proximity with the leaders dragged him into the politics also.

Harnam was his class fellow and a good old friend. Sharad dragged him too into the publication business. Harnam was happy in his motor spare parts business but when he saw his friend Sharad making millions in publication line, he was lured.

In business, a man is easily attracted towards another's glittering trade. Moreover in the motor market, there was a cut-throat competition now and profit margin was also falling. In Harnam's mind, the literary tickle was disturbing him. When he starting mixing more with Sharad, this itch was heightened.

Harnam wound up his motor spare parts shop and sold the stock at throwaway prices. He set up a brand new press at his residence.

With some clues from Sharad, he got good orders in the first year of his business but then people expected work on credit from him. Harnam's working capital was used up in a year. His debts were increasing.

The government officials took bribes from him and placed orders. They took the stocks but cheques remained pending because of lack of funds in the government circles. A large number of firms took the supply but when the time to pay came near, these people made excuses and pretexts of all kinds.

Harnam proved quite a novice in this trade. Within a year, his fifty lakhs were reduced to three lakhs.

When Harnam met Sharad in the country club last month, he demanded five lakhs from him. Sharad showed his inability and told him that his wife controlled the finances of the whole business.

Harnam begged from him that he had to pay for paper worth two lakhs failing which he would have to shut his business. Harnam said that it was a matter of few months now. From the next year, good business cycle would start, the government would change and the power would come in the hands of his known people. They would get the authority to spend, then the stock would be cleared and the pending bills would also be realised. He requested Sharad to lend him two lakh rupees and save him.

Sharad helped him by paying him the money from his credit card. The payment of higher rates of interest on credit card was decided to be paid by Harnam himself along with the principal amount.

Who knew that Harnam will pass away after two months, leaving Sharad in such a lurch? He passed away in his sleep due to a cardiac arrest.

Today everyone attending his funeral was praising him as an honest businessman and a good gentleman. Only good people get such a painless and easy death, they agreed.

But it was only Sharad who knew the reality of Harnam's honesty. How will Sharad pay such a heavy interest on the money taken by Harnam? He heaved a deep sigh.

The flames of Harnam's pyre were rising very high. After the last rites, everyone was given a small piece of sandalwood. It was a sort of ceremony in which the mourners present at the funeral place made a last circle of the burning pyre and throw the piece of sandalwood in the fire as a token of condolence and respect to the dead.

Sharad was encircling the fire and suddenly he observed a weird thing. At the end of a burning log of wood, an army of black ants was running out at a great speed to save itself from the fire. The piece of wood was not completely dry and possibly it was the home to small ants.

Sharad's morale went further down. He thought that his friend Harnam was so ill-fated and damned that he was not able to get a good quality of dry wood for his pyre.

Back home, Sharad could not sleep the whole night.

In the morning, he didn't go to his showroom. Instead, he headed towards the timber market. He purchased two tonnes of good quality sandalwood and kept it in his store.

He made his will stating that when he would die, his corpse should be burnt with that sandalwood.

When his wife learnt this, she went mad with anger. She roared, "Who gave you the right to block two lakhs of rupees on the sandalwood meant for pyre? You are quite hale and hearty."

Sharad told her the whole story right from his lending of money to Harnam and the strange incident at his funeral.

More than five years passed and Sharad completely forgot about Harnam. Now his business was expanding to other countries too.

These days, his eyes were on the coming Parliamentary Elections. He had secretly given twenty millions to the Party Headquarters and he was given the party ticket.

During an election campaign, Sharad was returning from his constituency one evening. His mobile rang.

His wife was on the other end. She chirped, "Only this morning the famous business tycoon Ghanshyam Dass died. I got a call from Rama Timber Store. They said that they are facing a shortage of sandalwood and require some for the pyre of the dead. There has been a ban on the wood felling in Assam and after the death of sandalwood smuggler Dacoit Veerappan, the rates of sandalwood have increased twenty times. They knew that you had purchased two tonnes of sandalwood from them five years back. Oh! You forgot. You remember the death of your dear friend Harnam who owed you more than two lakh rupees. Ya, that fellow. I sold back them that sandalwood at the prevailing rates. We have made a profit of thirty lakhs through that. It seems that your friend Harnam has paid back his loan along with a handsome interest."

Remembering the sad demise of his closest friend Harnam now, tears rolled down Sharad's eyes for the first time.

∞

The Return of Uncle Sam

It was a wonderful day of my life. I was riding in the city with Satish Uncle whom we all called Uncle Sam. Sitting in his brand new luxury car was a great fun for a common man like me. It was as if I was wandering in a dreamland.

Uncle Sam was in United States for the past twenty years. Whenever he visited us he brought costly, luxurious and charming gifts. With him prospering in United States, we all had nourished a hope that Uncle Sam would call us one by one and we all will settle there one day.

To our surprise, Uncle Sam retuned to India all of a sudden. All our cherished dreams and expectations were shattered.

We were fuming and fretting. Out of mounting curiosity I asked him, "Uncle Sam, there is a great rush of people wishing to go to America. There are unlimited chances of acquiring riches there. America is the only cherished destination of budding immigrants the entire world over. It is beyond my apprehension as to why you left that paradise and came to settle in a country like India. I can't digest all this. You know better that in India there is *jungle raj* everywhere. There is political instability all over and the infrastructure is so poor. Above all, there is corruption in every field. In these conditions, you won't get that rate of return over here."

I was looking at him in great consternation. Why did he decide to come here with full bag and baggage? There is no comparison of India with America.

Even our Ministers bow before the people settled in America. Last year, when Bill Clinton came here, Chief Ministers of more than a dozen states lined up like beggars before him requesting him to invest in their states. The biggest problem in India is that you can't trust anyone here in the matter of business. The condition of courts is horrific. Keeping in view all this, a person who is well-settled in America may not prosper in business here.

I was looking at Uncle Sam with great inquisitiveness. He guessed immediately what was going in my mind.

Pampering me and feeling like a king he spoke, "My dear boy, you are still living in the era of slow and dark fifties. You should be aware of what is happening all around. You do not know that the Modern India has a totally different look now. Frauds, scams, cheatings and plundering have become a thing of common occurrence here. Years ago these things were acceptable in advanced countries only. But now the poor nations have started providing these facilities to the shrewd businessmen."

With gleaming eyes he continued, "For a businessman, India is the right place now. No one listens to the voice of inner conscience here, though there is much talk about it all around. Here one can easily allure the corrupt and gullible officers and crooked political heads for a paltry sum. All the smart multinational corporations the world over have set their gluttonous eyes on India now. Look at the teeming millions here swarming like ants. To provide them bread, butter, clothes, house, cars, wine, mobile and petty jobs will be a business of profit worth billions of rupees. There is no rule and regulation here. Courts and police are on the side of the rich and the influential. Khaki and Khadi listen to the affluent person. What is there in America now? There is so much of strictness there. I have lived with many constraints for long, now I crave for some freedom. That's why I disposed off everything there and have come to India now. It is a promising land for the dreamers now. The history repeats itself. Many centuries ago, plunderers came and flourished here. Now I will re-assert and re-establish myself in India."

I was dumb with awe and admiration due to my lack of awakening about this new India. Uncle Sam had to visit a few government offices in connection with some licenses and approvals. First of all, we entered a small office. The furniture there was of British period. On most of the chairs, shabby coats of truant officials were hung.

Only four or five persons were running the whole office. Their faces were dry, eyes seemed dull and greedy and their stomachs were shrunk like those of hungry hounds. Their eyes shone when someone visited them personally for his work.

Uncle Sam enquired about his work from them. He was told that the concerned official was on a long leave. Moreover, there were many loopholes in Uncle Sam's application and many essential documents were to be attached.

No one was taking interest in his work. The Sectional Head created even more complications for him. His logic was not comprehensible to Uncle Sam and what Uncle Sam proposed was not clear to him.

The reality was different. These guys were trying to hook him for bribe. Though Uncle Sam was not a novice yet he was judging these corrupt officials' demands.

He took one person to the open terrace and with broad smile he asked him, "Yes man! Tell me frankly how all this mess can be cleared and how my work can be done today."

The official gave a meaningful smile and told him his rate. Uncle Sam handed him the money in brand new currency. And lo! His work and papers were ready in a few seconds! Uncle Sam got all the documents hand delivered by paying extra money to the dispatcher.

Now this had become the success mantra for Uncle Sam everywhere, "Yes man! How it can be done?" Wow! How pleasing and rewarding for both the sides! Pay the convenience fee and get any complicated job done within no time. One should know the right price for the favour asked.

That day Uncle Sam had a score of tasks in government and private offices. Everywhere his work *funda* was the same. He greased their palms and got through his work within seconds.

Those jobs requiring months of procedural delays and other complications were accomplished in half an hour. Uncle Sam crossed all the hurdles with the blessings of Laxmi, the Goddess of riches.

We headed towards the opulent bar and enjoyed chilled beer with roasted chicken. Uncle Sam was right in his opinion about 21st century India. Rightly it belongs to the privileged class.

In a social gathering, I met Uncle Sam after a gap of two years. I was stunned to see his vast empire. He had captured many vital fields of businesses.

Hugging me affectionately, he said, “Didn’t I say that India has become a much fertile land for outsiders? Don’t worry, I haven’t forgotten you. For you too, I have a first-rate plan in my mind. I am thinking about starting a good newspaper. A daily is essential for a business magnate like me. There he puts a lot of pressure on the Government through this and sways the ruling party in his favour. Now you will have to look after everything. Hey man! How it can be done?”

I was overjoyed. I was delighted to hear the same success mantra once again. I readily gave my approval.

Walking Down the Nostalgia Lane

How long someone could have waited for him?

He had unreasonably delayed his visit to that city. Hundreds of young men had migrated to other large cities in search of better job avenues. All the girls he knew were married off. The old men he was acquainted with were no more. God knows, where the boys he played with in his childhood were.

It was after forty long years, he came back here. Forty years is a long period, long enough in which not only the history but also the geography of a city changes completely.

He came well prepared from Delhi itself. For a comfortable stay in his old town, he had procured a recommendation letter in the name of the Principal of Navodaya Vidhyalaya of Nawanshahr from his friend who was the Deputy Director in Delhi. The Deputy Director had made a phone call to the Principal, personally urging him to make the stay of Suresh comfortable. Suresh was anxious about his stay since he knew no one in the town and he was not sure whether any good hotels were available there or not. This town was on a link road, away from the main Grand Trunk Road.

When he entered the town, his mind changed. On the outer area of the town, he saw a number of luxurious hotels. The vast and gorgeous hotel complex of Punjab Tourism titled *Chandni* fascinated him at the first sight. He ordered his driver to take his car inside it.

After checking in the hotel room, he changed his clothes. For the last eight hours, he was in the car. He was badly tired. His legs ached but his heart was excited. He had reached Nawanshahr at last.

For the last thirty years, he had been making plans to go to Nawanshahr but could not dare or will it so strongly. Though he had gone to Kolkata, Mumbai, Chennai, Dhaka, Tokyo and many far-off places, but going to Nawanshahr remained his long cherished dream. Being the Under-Secretary in the Ministry of Foreign Affairs, he had this advantage that he had made many foreign trips.

This city was upsetting him for the past so many years. It was repeatedly disturbing him in his dreams. All the night sometimes, he was roving in the old streets of this city where he roamed in his early days of life. He wandered plucking raw mangoes from Rehman's mango groves by climbing on the broken walls of the school boundary or eating *samosas* of *Kesar Mithaiwala* or buying pencils from Master Om Prakash's stationery shop or watching a movie at Mohan Talkies. He became upset.

To get rid of all that, this time Suresh decided to visit Nawanshahr.

So many recollections linked with his ancestral house had been tormenting him. It was the place where he took birth and studied up to tenth class. He always thought of visiting this place at least once in his lifetime but he was so busy with the work in the office that this dream visit was delayed for the past so many years.

He mentioned about all this torment to his wife and asked her to accompany him. She laughed dryly and remarked, "Those who have to go anywhere, don't waste time in seeking advices and asking for company of others. One fine morning, they pack up and go. You feel nostalgia for Nawanshahr. Go and satisfy it. We would be bored there."

Today he was standing in that city. His heart was pounding heavily and he wanted to go to that small oblivious village where once his family lived.

Seeing the cold faces and strange people, a bizarre thought came to his mind. This city had expired for him long time back. They had gone from here a long ago. What was he searching here now?

He again thought that maybe the city is alive but he died for her some forty years back and was born again in Delhi.

He was excited at the very idea to have reached and roaming around the place for which he was pining so passionately. He promised himself that from now, he would come here every year and will bring his wife and children too.

He tried to imagine – will everything be in the same old state as it was at the time he left? He laughed at his foolishness. It was preposterous to think that the world would have stopped where he had left it. He himself had changed a lot. There was a sea change in his outlook, his thinking, his lifestyle and his priorities. Philosophers rightly say that only change is a permanent thing in this world. He would have forgotten about this city completely but it remained fresh in his memory for the fact that it was tormenting him in his dreams.

In the partition of 1947, his parents had migrated to Nawanshahr from a small village of Lahore. They were allotted land here in a small dusty village near Nawanshahr. Namanshahr was a sleepy backward town – a remote *tehsil* of Jalandhar District in Punjab state.

In those days, the people of this area had a strong fascination to go and settle in Delhi. It was their dream destination. A number of relatives of these migrated people lived in the areas of West Delhi like Tilak Nagar, Punjabi Bagh and Kingsway Camp. It was very easy in those days to get a job or to start a small business there.

Suresh completed his Higher Secondary Examinations and applied for clerical post. He prepared hard for the competitive tests and soon got a job in a Ministry at Delhi. He was still a young boy of nineteen years. How could he live in Delhi all alone?

He planned in such a way that within three years, all his family members shifted to Delhi. His father had a small field. They gave their land on contract farming. Suresh's younger brother was not good at studies. He was stuck in tenth class for the last two years. So he had him employed as a helper at a mechanic shop in Delhi. Within a year, his brother learnt the job and started earning.

Suresh arranged the marriages of his two sisters here. Then he was married. He chose a working woman as a life partner. By dint of hard work, he rose to the post of Class One Officer. He left Nawanshahr for good. All other relatives too, migrated to other places.

In the 1984 riots, all other known persons and distant relatives left the village and then Suresh and his family never went back there again. His father sold the land and the old house at throwaway prices. So every link from this place was broken at last. Now once again, he was there to enliven all that which transpired forty years ago.

Reaching the hotel, he started thinking about his strategy to visit all the places in one day since he had a tight schedule in Delhi. The Principal of Navodaya Vidhyalaya, Mr. Joshi lived in Ram Nagar colony. Suresh phoned him.

Mr. Joshi told him that he had made the arrangements for his stay in a government rest house. Suresh promised to see Mr. Joshi in the morning.

Suresh set out to leave his driver at the rest house. He made his arrangements there and came back in his car. On his way back to the Punjab Tourism Hotel, Suresh could not control himself. He thought of paying a visit to his ancestral village which was just two miles from the main bus stand.

He took the road to his village. On both the sides, standing crops of mustard bloomed yellow and sugarcane spread sweetness in the air. The village had undergone a complete transformation in the last forty years. His heart was pounding heavily as he took the left turn on the road leading to the village.

He had barely gone one mile that he forgot the way. The roads had changed beyond recognition. There were new residential colonies all around. Markets and shops were realigned. Old structures had given place to the new. Electricity, tractors, automobiles, phones and mobiles had entered the otherwise quiet and sleepy village.

The old lonely road that was alive in his memory was nowhere to be found. It was pitch dark outside. He was not known to any person. From whom and about whom he could have enquired?

He was disappointed. He returned back with the resolve that with Mr. Joshi he would go there in the morning and try to locate his roots. He reached the hotel and took two large pegs of wine, had his dinner and slept. For the first time, he had a sound sleep. He was not troubled by any old memory or unusual nightmare.

In the morning, the phone call of his driver woke him. He got ready and within an hour, he was at the residence of Mr. Joshi. He took his breakfast there.

Suresh said cheerfully, "Well sir, from where should we start? I have one full day today. I want to visit Government Primary School of Kishan Garh, *Naugajja Peer*, *tehsil* complex, Government Senior Secondary School Nawanshahr, nearby hills of Saketi…"

Mr. Joshi said in a calm voice, "My son, this is a very small town. You have a car. You will ramble everywhere in three hours only."

Becoming sober, he remarked, "Your ancestral village Kishan Garh has lost its past identity completely. The refugees who had come from Pakistan in 1947 have all gone to Delhi, Ambala and other towns of Haryana during the riots of 1984. Now there are barely ten-twelve houses of original residents.

The growing city has engulfed the village and its sprawling land. Now the village has become a part of the city itself."

He continued, "In 1984 riots, the rates of the land were ten thousand rupees per acre and now the rates are touching ten millions per acre. The village was considered to be backward then but now it is the posh area of the town with grand shopping malls and magnificent showrooms. It is all a matter of time. Time is all pervasive."

Turning towards Suresh, he said, "Now go and see all you wanted to see. When we don't have any known persons to visit in particular, then it doesn't take much time to roam and see the city. After you finish, your dinner is fixed with us."

Mr. Joshi sent a teacher with him. First of all, they headed towards the Government School in the city itself. Suresh had his high schooling here. He wanted to see some old records. He walked proudly in all the rooms. The whole design was different now. New building had been erected in the place of old one. All the teachers were new. They were unknown to the names put forth by Suresh. He could not get any clue about his batch mates.

But that was not all in which he was interested. He wanted to satisfy his curiosity about his past days and forlorn places.

They headed towards the area where there used to be his house. On the way, he saw the same *Kesar Mithaiwala's* shop but now its name was *Kesar's Fast Food*. It resembled a popular café. There was hustle and bustle there. Just near it, there used to be the *Billu's* tailoring shop and to the left there was the famous stationery shop of Master Om Prakash.

Everything had changed. The thing that Suresh was searching out was nowhere to be found. The face, contour, shape, taste and colour of all the forty-year-old things and places had undergone a complete metamorphosis. Had he been visiting this place off and on then he could have preserved the missing links of the changing town. But he was absent from here.

Suresh was disenchanted. The place where he spent the prime nineteen years of his life looked quite unknown, unfamiliar and stranger to him. This was what he was meandering unnecessarily in his dreams. This was the ghost which took his peace of mind for the past so many years.

There was nothing nostalgic about it. No traces of the glorious period. What is here to long for now? No known one, no old companion. He lost all the vigour. He was a fool to think that he would come here every year.

The building of the primary school was not there. Instead, a well-planned residential colony had taken its place. Suresh wondered that when he left the village, the village too deserted and cheated him. It scratched his past and destroyed all the memories relating to his life. Nothing was left here to feel about.

With a distressing mood, he headed towards Delhi the next morning. He was thinking what he would narrate to his wife regarding his bitter experiences there. He was frustrated all the more and thought that he wasted so much time and energy in fulfilling his nostalgic whims.

Till now, he had a firm belief that his childhood memories were placed safe somewhere and one day he would find time and leisure to go and cherish them. But now he felt that even his childhood was snatched from him. Suresh was no doubt unfaithful to his birthplace but his village had proved disloyal too.

The Unending War

Leaving Deepa at the Quality Hotel, I came back and went to the kitchen to prepare tea for myself.

I asked mom, "Would you like to accompany me?"

She was irritated. She asked, "Where has Deepa gone? When will she come back?"

This is the same old eccentric nature of mom. She will go on enquiring about every petty thing happening in the house. Moreover, these days it has become a strange habit of mom to ask about the same thing a number of times. She does it deliberately or being aged, she forgets what is told to her, I can't make out easily.

Just an hour before when Deepa was getting ready, I had told mom that today was Deepa's kitty party at a hotel. Now again, I will have to explain all the things to mom.

I controlled my temper and told her, "Just an hour ago I had told you that Deepa is going to the hotel in her kitty party. She will take lunch there. They hold a committee type of gathering and the lady, who gets the committee, gives party to her friends. I am making tea, will you like to take?"

Mom easily finds an occasion to offend me. She said in an annoying mood, "Why do you take tea all the time? Take some milk instead. Your health will improve. In this city, everyone takes tea anytime. Even before meals or at midnight. Is tea some tonic?"

I entered the kitchen without uttering a single word. I had no reply of many illogical questions of mom. Even in my dreams, I don't want to offend her. As per my dear wife Deepa, I am the most submissive creature on earth.

And mom knows my weakness and due to that, she scolds me in the presence of Deepa and also snubs her in my presence.

It is only I who knows that mom has passed his whole life in the midst of illiterate villagers and poor farmers. She doesn't have refined mannerisms. She doesn't know how to talk cleverly and tactfully. She tells everything openly at the face.

Deepa was born and brought up in a metropolitan city. Here, there are no reservations. Her parents are well-educated and she is from a rich family.

Deepa becomes angry at the orthodox verbal volleys of mom many times. She quarrels with her. At most occasions, there starts a cold war between them.

In some matters, I persuade her, "Deepu dear, mom has to stay here just for a month. She has no malice or ill-will for you in her mind. Please try to understand her. You are a post graduate in psychology. Mom's excessive concern for us has made her like this. Moreover, she lives alone in a small town and has developed this bad habit of interfering and taunting us. Try to accommodate with her."

Sometimes Deepa's tolerance gives way. It happens like this; mom gets angry or gives useless advices to Deepa. Deepa feels choked inside but doesn't say anything to her though she wants. But she holds back to avoid lest matter goes out of control. She fumes and frets, but doesn't argue with mom. She becomes tight-lipped and goes on doing her work."

Mom gets angrier due to this. When she gets no answer to her arguments, she gets more upset and furious. Moreover, she always finds a way to find a defect in Deepa's cooking, social relationships, our lifestyle or our system of spending.

The same thing happened on that day. There came a bowlful of pudding from the house of Deepa's friend Hina. Deepa offered it to mom first.

Mom keeps all the information. She asked, "When did you cook the pudding?"

Though Deepa had forbidden me to tell but I spoke at once, "Mom, this has come from the house of Hina, Deepa's friend."

It was only after the impact that I realised my mistake. Hina belongs to a Muslim family. Mom does not eat anything brought from her house.

She got a new issue to grill us, "Why are you bent upon maligning your religion? Being a Hindu you…"

I took the centre stage openly, "Mom, the world has changed completely these days. These people whom you discard are very sophisticated, hygienic and neat. At least, they are far better than Sardari Lal, our distant relative, in whose house you take lunch and dinner. Many times we saw fungus on their utensils. Hina belongs to a well-to-do and modern family."

I thought I was too harsh on mom. I took a different turn, "Mom, you yourself were telling that during the partition of 1947, your neighbour in a village near Lahore, helped you a lot. He guarded your valuables well. Two months after the riots, you went and brought your things back."

I made a clean sweep. Here, mom felt defenceless. Tears rolled down her eyes. She became emotional. The sad memories of her native place came to her mind.

With deep voice she said, "Those people were very nice. When we departed, they were weeping bitterly. There was my childhood friend, Salma. She embraced me so tightly. She was not letting me go. She was weeping badly and saying – don't go, take to my religion instead or carry me with you. Don't take life out of me."

One day mom said, "Birju of our town lives here. Let us visit him one day."

I wanted to avoid him. He lived in Old Delhi. There is great rush there. Going there means wasting a full day. Mom couldn't go there all alone.

I made an excuse, "Mom, what will you do there? He is a third rate man. One day, he met me in Karol Bagh. He was drunk in the broad day light. After all he is a bus driver..."

Mom got angry, "Everyone drinks these days. And you too, go to those cocktail parties. We should socialise with known people from our side."

Becoming more irritated, she went on, "You have distanced yourself from everyone after coming here. When you will hold the function of the marriage of your children, then who will come to your door?"

Here, she started attacking at my weak points. I said, "Mom, I didn't mean this…"

Mom was shelling bombs, "I know what you mean and what you don't mean. I have seen the world. I am not a fool. You people got education, good job, got an educated earning wife and built a house here and that means you have become big. And all others are just pawns and small before you."

She went on and on, "Small town relatives are your real sympathisers. They will stand by you through thick and thin. In city, your branches have grown out but your real roots are in the village only. You will have to return there. One day, you will realise that what is here was just a mirage…."

Now the moment had come where I thought that everything would have to be told clearly. I said with a firm mind, "Look mom, I faced so many difficulties and got education by living in a rented accommodation in city, toiling day and night. My kids can't go back to a small town in which our ancestors lived. I and Deepa have jobs here. How then we will go back to the roots? We have grown here. Now try to understand this. You should also stay here now. Only then we can look after you well. There are better facilities and medical services here. And moreover, I get upset when you stay there for months."

Mom justified herself unnecessarily, "How can I live here in peace? I can't live like a prisoner. No one talks to me freely. There is dead ice in the neighbourhood. No one comes out and goes to each other's house. I am afraid if I stay here for a year, I will forget my language. What an artificial life! But you have those values in your rearing. You should stay connected with your own people and think of building a house near our land."

I became mum. I was not ready for these preposterous alternatives. We had our own problems and priorities. I had recently bought a luxury car. Its instalments were going. he kids were in a good school. Their expenses were rising.

We were thinking of selling this flat and buying a penthouse. How could I think of building a house in my remote village and for whom? Just to please mom? No way!

In our scheme of things, mom's suggestion looked odd and out of place. She gets no companion here, it was a fact. She should familiarise herself with other channels of communications.

But barely a month after coming to my place, she gets ready to go back to her town.

Deepa cannot not understand her. On which things mom gets annoyed and on which thing she becomes happy, it is always unpredictable and a puzzle. She is hard to please.

When we admitted our elder daughter in a famous dance school, mom reacted cynically. In a city like ours, it was a great privilege to get admission there. She had a great career in that.

Mom was here in Delhi when she learned. She raised the sky on her head. She said, "A girl has to go to her in-laws' house after all. What is the logic in spending so much on her? Teach her household job and sewing etc. This dancing is beyond my comprehension."

On hearing such out of place bits of advices and scolding from mom, Deepa went out of that room. I was left there alone to argue with mom. Though, I too was reared in those outdated values and adverse circumstances but at this period of time in 21st century, new lifestyle, new values, practical way of thinking and living have conditioned me and I completely condemn what used to happen in the past. I started professing in favour of a new way of living and a scientific outlook. Then an unending conversation opened between me and mom which led us nowhere.

Now or Never

He was placed on gate duty again and that too second time this week. Deepak asked the monitors of X-A and VIII-B, "Why am I given this cruel job of checking every other day?"

The girls shrugged their shoulders and remarked, "What can we say, sir?"

Deepak started strolling from one end to another. He was wondering why the classes were not returning from the morning assembly.

The Principal Madam must definitely be giving the students an appealing and heartrending lecture on honesty, duty, discipline and what not. And she herself is a woman of double standards.

She is always ready to accommodate a rich boy seeking an admission in her school. She never bothers about his past performance. Her mouth starts watering if the parents are affluent and are prepared to give a handsome donation to her.

She says, "Right, you may submit the transfer certificate later on. Take admission quickly. To improve his grades, I will put him in special coaching classes which are held in the morning before the start of the school for which we charge extra."

These unwanted and unworthy students who are shunted away from all schools are too difficult to tackle. Teaching this discarded stuff and showing good result is the most difficult job in this world. The hands of the teachers ache caning them and their throats get parched while shouting at them but there is no improvement in these useless fellows. All are of the same category – careless, vagabonds, dull and pigheaded. Most of them don't attend school for weeks.

In the parents-teacher meeting, the Principal Madam snubs the parents of these worthless students. She says cleverly, "Look sir, when we can't bring about any improvement in your child, we don't deserve to take such heavy fees from you."

The parents become depressed and shameful to realise that they are not effective enough to send their children regularly and on time to school, leave aside the grades in tests. The children should not roam unnecessarily, absenting themselves from the school. The Principal instils this sense of guilt in the minds of the parents and gets scot-free from her responsibility.

The parents have neither time nor any expertise to guide their children. Some of them are small and medium shopkeepers, petty government officials and people engaged in transport and other petty services. Principal Madam interacts with these shy people in fluent English and then every month collects heavy tuition fees from them with express right.

While pursuing graduation in Science, Deepak had never thought even in his dreams that at the end he will get this petty job of teaching in a private school. His father sent him to the college facing great hardships. He had a petty job of accounts as a clerk in a private firm. Though their family was small but they lived in a rented house and with a cashier's job, they had little means at their end.

Deepak was intelligent. He got through every class with good marks, so no one stopped him from pursuing higher studies. After graduation, he was forced to seek a job so that he could support the family.

There was widespread corruption all around. For one post, thousands came forward. Deepak had neither high links nor money to offer. He faced many competitive examinations but he was not selected even for a clerical post. He spent so much money in filling job applications. He had no resources for getting a coaching, purchasing guides and procuring other helpful material.

He went from pillar to post, did tuitions and jobs in various other schools and after hankering at so many places, he was now in this recognised private high school.

The school resembled a pigeon box. It was like an old prison cell. In a four-storey building, the entire school of ten classes with different sections was securely stocked. The roofs were low, and rooms were 8×10 with little ventilation. The benches were very small so that more students could be accommodated in a room.

The school was located in the middle of the busiest market. The high-pitched noise of hawkers, street vendors, fast moving vehicles making piercing sounds, the shooting noise from the adjoining classrooms was irritating. Listening to all that, when he joined, Deepak had thought that he would go mad one day. But now, he had become used to all this humbug.

In the beginning, Deepak was not only hopeful but dead sure that he would leave this school one day for a better job elsewhere. He was holding a science degree with first class. But he had bitter experiences striving hard for a good job. He was convinced that these days, good jobs were reserved only for those with money or political links. Rest of the people were destined to do petty private jobs. That is why he had distanced himself away from all sorts of competitions and preparations.

His co-teacher Sandeep whom all popularly called *Maths Sir* had made a stunning progress despite the fact that he had joined the school much later than Deepak.

Deepak remained idealistic but *Maths Sir* opened a coaching centre though the school authorities had put a ban on that. Deepak obeyed the rules but *Maths Sir* took a room away from his house and was secretly and successfully running his coaching centre. More than fifty students from the school itself attended his tuition centre in the evening.

The *Maths Sir* had purchased a brand new car last month. He wore branded clothes and conversed frankly. He would prank with every young and smart teacher of the school. He even had a romantic involvement with a girl of a rich family who was in tenth class. Deepak felt jealous of him.

Deepak thought he was doomed to this wretched life for ever. There was no ray of hope now. When he was young, he was always worried about the completion of his studies. Then he struggled to get a job. Now at least he had a job but still he did not find himself associated to anybody.

Of course, once in his life, he had developed a close affinity with Sunanda. She had joined this school after doing her graduation. She belonged to a well-to-do family and was planning to do B.Ed. She had joined this school for the sake of fun and to get an experience certificate of six months which was necessary to do B.Ed.

One day, Deepak and Sunanda were all alone in the staff room.

Sunanda told Deepak, "My mom says that the best thing in the world is a government job. No tension of any sort. The salary is attractive and no nonsense of the school management as it is here. After teaching for six months here, I will say you bye-bye. God knows when we shall meet again. From the new session, I will take admission in B.Ed. from Open University. My father has good connections in the Education Department. I will surely get a job. Should I try for you too, my Devdass?"

Deepak became depressed all the more. He thought that so many blessed guys had such foolproof plans for their bright future. And there was one like him who was just pulling on, floating on water. Current took him wherever it wanted to.

Sunanda was a very witty, sharp and broadminded girl having a ready sense of humour. She laughed loudly and played pranks on everyone. She made fun of the Principal Madam all the time. She called her 'Princy'. And then, all the teachers and many students started calling the Principal by this catchy name. *Maths Sir* hankered after her but she always knew his evil designs.

So she kept him at a distance right from the beginning. She had a soft corner for Deepak. She thought him to be sincere, truthful and brilliant.

One day Sunanda and Deepak were sitting in the staff room. It was their zero period. They were discussing the syllabus for the half yearly examinations.

Deepak summoned courage to tell her his true feelings. He said, "Sunanda, won't you remember us when you will leave this school?"

She said in a humorous mood, "You said nothing that I should remember."

"If I dare say it now, would you reply in a good spirit?'

'Yes, I will. Let me see your dare first."

"Well, I think you know it."

"I know so many things but I want to hear from your mouth."

"Sometimes you talk so affectionately that I find you quite close to my heart but sometimes you drive me far away. I cannot understand your true feelings for me."

"Listen to what your heart says and that will be the final answer."

"My heart is not in my control these days. It has different explanations every day. And today it has left the judgement on you."

"Life doesn't go with a perpetual puzzle. I think you are afraid to accept the reality."

"What is that? You don't take anything serious. I fear if I will tell you something, you will make fun of me."

Sunanda said boldly, "I tell you frankly. I make fun of you in front of others but in my heart I feel that you are a very sincere fellow...."

Suddenly *Maths Sir* entered. Both got nervous. Deepak blushed as if he was caught stealing something.

Maths Sir knew that something romantic was cooking between the two. He also knew that Deepak won't be able to say about his love to Sunanda since he was a sentimental fool. He was a victim of inferiority complex though he was a brilliant boy.

Maths Sir commented sarcastically, "Deepak Sir, the weather is very romantic today. I think, a moment ago both of you were chirping like Romeo and Juliet. Now you look sad when I entered. Sir, say quickly what you want to say since Sunanda is leaving next month."

Pat came the reply from Sunanda, "I smell something burning."

Maths Sir was snubbed. She went on further, "You take care of yourself. You are going very dangerously these days. The day the news of your affair with your student Veena Sethi reaches the ears of Princy, she will clip off your wings. All your tuition business will come down like a house of cards."

She always remained serious with Deepak. She would guide him to look smart and dress well. She also advised him not to remain depressed.

One day she said, "You are such a genius. Why don't you start a coaching centre at your home?"

Deepak found a clue, "The Princy is against it. She runs the coaching classes in the school itself. Will you join me if I start some new venture? I will have to leave this job."

Sunanda said, "The day I complete my B.Ed. I will come to you first. Then we will decide."

One day Deepak was combing his hair, looking in the mirror hung on the wall of III-C. Sunanda saw him and remarked lovingly, "Okay, it is enough now. You are already so smart and cute, there is no need to make more efforts. I don't want someone else to fix her design on you."

God knows how much serious was Sunanda but Deepak was in the air for a few days.

She didn't join the school in the new session. Deepak kept waiting for her. It was only she in whom he saw some hope of a new life.

He thought many times that he should go to her house and enquire about her but he could not dare. He thought what he would answer to her parents' queries. Sunanda disappeared completely and Deepak too forgot her.

He could not go well the way other teachers prospered. He saw the school solely as a centre of business. In his days, teachers had a good moral character and the students were motivated by them but now there was no ideal for them.

The schools had become a commercial centre where education was imparted through readymade notes. Students just mugged up important questions and in exams too, the teachers helped them cheat and copy. No one studies from the textbooks. Guides, help books and tuition notes were used in all the classes.

The Princy lay stress on one thing only, "Revise important topics numerous times. The students should get good marks. I have to show these marks to their parents. In the 8th and 10th standard, two or three students should bag merit positions. Do whatever is possible. Bribe the outside invigilators, I don't care for money but the name of this school should shine."

The main emphasis was on two things only — cleanliness and discipline. If any student was late or absent from school, the only punishment was 'fine'. Not only this, there was a provision of heavy fine for not doing homework, not taking school test and especially not buying a particular book prescribed by the teacher. In this way, the school earned a good amount by way of fines.

In the name of cleanliness too, heavy fines were imposed. There was a tight and foolproof arrangement for this. The assembly was held in the adjoining municipality park since the school had no ground of its own. Before the close of prayer session, the main gate of the school's building was closed.

By rotation, the duties of one teacher and two monitors of different classes were fixed daily to conduct this exercise of checking personal hygiene of the student. In a register, the names of the defaulters were noted down and fine was collected. If some student failed to pay the fine on the spot, his name was written in the memo book. The amount due was then collected later on or along with the fees.

Detailed checking was carried out in respect of each child. His uniform, socks, school shoes, clean hankie, tie, belt, hair band, nails, clean teeth etc. all were checked. If any of these things was found to be missing or improper, a fine of one rupee for each default was imposed.

Whenever Deepak was assigned the duty at this fine barrier, he got upset and depressed seeing the plight of students of poor families. These students brought some pocket money in order to buy some refreshments in the recess but these clever and greedy management people and their head Princy, robbed their petty amount. With these fines, she had made this big empire. Only last week, she bought another Mercedes car.

Today the classes were definitely delayed for no obvious reasons. Deepak then remembered, "Oh! It is the teacher's day. Today, what more a teacher can give to his pupil except his discourse. The education is auctioned now. Whosoever bids for the higher price, gets it. Today the Princy must be in high spirits. She must be giving a long and impressive lecture to them — honesty, duty, values and obedience. Pity! Words are louder than deeds."

The classes were now about to enter the gate. One half of the gate was closed and the monitors on duty stood in the middle of the second half of the main gate. The students entered one by one. The checking monitors started their daily exercise of scrutiny. Tie, hankie, school uniform, black shoes, teeth, nails etc. were being examined and fine was being collected.

Deepak was supervising the job. Suddenly he glanced at a one rupee coin on the delicate palm of a frail student. The checking monitors were scolding him to take out one more coin from his pocket but he told them that the coin slipped out since his pocket was torn.

A checking monitor slapped him saying that he was telling a lie. The boy started weeping. He was saying, "Believe me, I am not a liar."

The second monitor got hold of him. Pulling his hair mercilessly, she made him stand on one side and called Deepak to intervene.

Seeing such high-handedness, Deepak could not control himself. He came forward.

He took the first bold decision of his life.

He flung opened the other half of the gate and announced in a loud voice, "Today is the teacher's day. So, no checking. Go, enjoy yourself."

The checking monitors looked at him flabbergasted. Nothing of this sort had ever happened in the history of Blooms Model School.

Even Deepak's legs were trembling at his foolish behaviour lest Princy would fire him from the job. But when he saw the students rushing in a jubilant mood, he was proud of his decision.

After fifteen minutes, he was standing before the Princy. She was scolding him badly. He had no idea how to react. He kept mum.

A voice came from the door, "I had said, when I will finish my B.Ed., I will come to you first. I kept my promise. Now, what do you say?"

The Princy changed her mood and remarked, "Welcome Sunanda, just now a vacancy has been created by Deepak. He is leaving. You may join the school here and now."

Sunanda said in her old ironic tone, "No, Princy, I give a damn to you. I have come to meet Mr. Deepak. Let us go, man."

They crossed the Princy's threshold and the one rupee fine barrier.

And then wings added to his gait.

Tambola Tricks

"Sweet Sixteen."

"*Murgi chor* is number Four."

Tambola was in full swing.

Kitty parties are very popular these days. There was a time when only urban elite class organised these sorts of flamboyant parties just to pass time and show each other their sprawling houses, expensive clothes and riches. Only sexy, smart and fashionably plump ladies were perfect in this game. Now these have become very common.

Uttering a number with a filthy sentence, Poonam laughed aloud and the other ladies joined her too.

Renu was irritated. She shouted, "Please don't do this, I'll miss my number. Poonam, shake the numbers well."

Neha and Mrs. Nagpal sat very close to each other. Their comic whispers were on.

"Always first is number One."

"*Mota Seth* is number Eight", said Poonam.

Neha remarked smilingly and meaningfully, "Why have you stopped saying now – one fat Major number Eight. Afraid of Mrs. Nagpal?"

Poonam answered nervously, "You know, last year in the kitty of Renu, Mrs. Nagpal took it bad when I said one fat Major number Eight. For many days she didn't speak to me. So I have changed it to *mota seth*."

Mrs. Nagpal said defensively, "No, no! The game is a game. I don't mind at all. Moreover my husband is a Brigadier now. Why should I mind for a bloody fat Major? Moreover, my hubby is quite slim and trim. He weighs just seventy kilograms."

Sweety remarked, "Mrs. Nagpal, you are saying with such assurance as if you weigh him daily."

Renu chirped, "After all, the weight of our husbands is no stranger to us."

All burst out loudly. Some elder ladies were smiling shyly.

Neha said, "Please, Poonam, finish this tambola quickly. I have to go early. You know my mother-in-law is with me these days."

Mrs. Nagpal remarked satirically, "Who fears the mothers-in-law these days? On the contrary, they are afraid of us."

Renu was sulking, "I too have to go early. I have to pick up my daughter from her school. Poonam, shake the numbers well and then announce."

Poonam shook the bowl violently. It contained large button-shaped plastic numbers.

She took out one and announced, "Tender age is Fourteen."

Sweety cried loudly, "Wow! My second line is finished."

"Come on, get it tallied from the numbers on the board."

Neha teased her, "Poonam, Sweety is a big cheater. Declare her boggy. It will be a great fun."

Sweety was notorious for cheating. She baffled a lot and had been caught many times. She was fussy and quarrelsome too.

Poonam matched her slip and this time found the number matching with the board. Sweety was given fifty rupees for the second line.

"Lovely legs is number Eleven."

Mrs. Nagpal's whispering was in full swing. She was cracking funny tit-bits and light jokes. Three ladies were bending over her. These ladies had more interest in her humorous volleys than in the tambola game.

Mrs. Nagpal was continuing, "You know, tambola is conducted very aptly by my friend Veena. Her style is so hilarious and amusing that while playing tambola with her, we laugh so boisterously that our bellies ache. By God, such dirty words she employs! You know, what she says to number one and sixty-nine, shit, I can't utter in the presence of the old aunties here. I will take you there one day and you will see her sharp and witty tongue. My goodness, even downmarket men must be more sophisticated in their tongue as compared to Veena. But we fully enjoy her obscene language."

Pushpa, rubbing her red hot nose said, "One more number and I will get the third line."

Sweety was attempting to match numbers of her slips with those placed on the tambola board.

Neha interrupted, "What is to be done regarding the pending amount of Mrs. Verma?"

Poonam's naughty son was playing with the unannounced numbers kept separately in the tumbler. The attention of most of the ladies was fixed up there lest he may lose any number which mattered to them. But etiquette was stopping them from scolding that impish boy.

Poonam took him to task, "Please my darling, *Mera Raja Beta*, go and play outside. Look there, all your new friends are around. Go and play with Nitin."

Renu suggested in a teacher's tone, "These kitties should be on Sundays. Men folks are around. At least they can take care of these rascal kids."

Neha was bent on having a decision regarding Mrs. Verma's unpaid kitty money. She said twice but no one listened.

Actually the ladies had taken for granted that there were no chances of Mrs. Verma's return or the pending amount. Her due share of pending kitties was treated by them as a bad debt. She had run away from the city and had taken the full amount of her kitty. Her husband's business was said to be running in loss, so they left the city silently one fine morning.

The whole epic of Mrs. Verma came to the centre stage.

"She didn't pay two month's rent to the landlord."

"She had a posh villa on a reasonable rent."

"She ditched us. How we will face her landlord now? I was interested to get that bungalow for my sister."

"Her husband's business was not that bad. My husband was saying that it was all a foul play. Mr. Verma wanted to change his business. He cheated his partner. Mrs. Verma too made a fool of many people and amassed good loot."

"The owner of Vansh departmental store, the Rohila confectionery and even the lady of New Looks Boutique, all made enquiries from me. I clearly said that Mrs. Verma was just our kitty member and nothing else. We don't know her new address. She owes fifty thousand as kitty money to us. If you find her, recover our money too. We will reward you suitably."

"People won't leave her."

"My husband says, give him a chance and he will locate those cheats."

"But how will we face her?"

"Poor unlucky fellows! Lost all the goodwill of fifteen years. Where they would have gone with this bad reputation?"

"Poor, my foot! She was very shrewd. How grand she lived!"

"She bought extravagant and expensive dresses every week."

"Lavish parties, daily cocktails."

"She had promised payments."

"She had sent one or two instalments through Poonam."

"Now Mrs. Nagpal, what is the share of our contribution to compensate for Mrs. Verma's loot?"

Mrs. Nagpal took out the diary and started counting and writing something in it.

Renu shrieked, "Poonam, finish the tambola. I will be late in this humbug."

Poonam took out one number at random, looked at it and satirically announced, "Badmash Number Ten."

Neha cried excitedly, "Third line please."

"Mix the numbers, very bad day today."

"Hey Ram! One number and the first house will be mine."

Poonam again started shouting like the usher standing outside a session court. Everyone was tense, holding breath, waiting for the wanted number. Their hearts were pumping heavily. The race to finish first and get a thousand rupee was going fast.

"Lucky number Seven."

"Two little ducks Twenty-two."

"Unlucky number Thirteen."

And the last game was over.

They were all exhausted.

Then they attacked on the dishes prepared by Poonam.

Mrs. Nagpal took only a spoonful of everything in her plate and said softly in the ears of Renu, "People order these things from the restaurant and boast that they had prepared these delicious dishes themselves. We aren't fools. We find out everything."

The whole group was now moving towards the gate. Mrs. Verma's betrayal was still the topic of discussion. The compensating amount which every member was paying each month because of her treachery was pinching everyone.

Some ladies were suspecting that since Poonam and Mrs. Verma were close friends, Mrs. Verma visited Poonam even now. When Mrs. Verma was a proclaimed offender, Poonam was not leaking out her secret and her new address since Mrs. Verma owed lakhs of rupees to the shopkeepers. A few women claimed that she was still in the city and they had seen her once in an exhibition and once in a shopping mall.

They had formed groups now. One group was discussing new trends of fashion, hairstyle, new boutique, salons and slimming centres. They cared little for money.

The other one was a religious-minded group which was exchanging notes on latest trend of yoga, worship, astrologers and religious gurus.

And yet another was a group of busy ladies whose children were in primary classes. They were here but their minds were in their household chores and errands.

Soon they were leaving one by one.

"Okay bye, Poonam. See you at Renu's kitty."

All voices sounded in one chorus. Mrs. Nagpal was the last one to go since she had developed a close affinity with Poonam these days.

Everyone had gone.

Poonam shut the main gate securely. She rushed upstairs.

Unlocking the door, she plunged into the sofa.

Mrs. Verma's face was pale and fatigued. She stopped turning the pages of the magazine. She was uneasy and nervous. She spoke in a depressing voice, "I heard them abusing me. Tell me what Mrs. Nagpal said. Just a few days more and I will come before them."

Poonam said in a nervous tone, "She went in the last. I told her the truth about you. I said her husband's business is going well now. In the next kitty, she will join us and will clear all her dues."

Mrs. Verma rubbed her sore moist eyes. Poonam cupped her cheeks. Tears gushed down. They say even crocodiles shed tears. It was only Mrs. Verma who knew that she was not in a position to face the public.

∞

If Winters Come

It was a record of the Jubilee Cinema House. Every film screened here was a super hit. Jubilee was a thing of envy and pride. In the morning, the school and college going kids would especially turn their bicycles towards it to have a glance at the posters of the film, currently screened or coming next. There was a hustle and bustle in its compound till late night. Jubilee shone and glittered in floodlight.

It was the pride of this town. In the circle of one hundred miles, there was no other Cinema Hall which could match it. Rajesh Khanna was a superstar in those days. His every film celebrated silver jubilee here. Many films had set the record of being a golden jubilee too. The cinema hall proved its name 'Jubilee' in the real sense of the term. There was no chance that one may confront a bore or any flop movie here.

Bobby was screened here. It drew a thunderous rush. People from the neighbouring states thronged the hall. Crazy boys were so fanatical to see this movie's first day first show that they tore trousers and shirts at the ticket window.

The persons who black-marketed its tickets became millionaires. A 20-rupee balcony ticket was sold in black for five hundred rupees. People watched the movie standing in dormitory. Such was the craze to watch movie at Jubilee those days.

Had someone informed the proprietors of Guinness World Records, we would have had many astonishing, rare and memorable records relating to Jubilee with us today. *Sholay* broke all previous records. It ran houseful for one whole year. People saw it many times. *Jai Santoshi Maa*, though being a religious movie, was a super-duper hit. It did a grand business for thirty weeks.

Jubilee was known for its luxurious soft-cushioned seats. Its air-conditioner was an incredible one. In those days, very few people had air coolers. Owners of B.D. Flour Mills and Jagdamba Soap Factory had air-conditioners at their homes. People were wonderstruck feeling the cool balcony and looking at the glittering interior of Jubilee.

There was precious wall to wall carpet all around and on the floor the mattress was remarkable. Place a foot on it and the person would sink one foot down. Tidy and shining walls and impressive getup made it look like a royal palace.

During interval, the scene at the lower stall canteen was one of a great strife. One bottle of cold drink could be grabbed at the price of rupees ten while in the market its cost was rupees five. But it was worth enjoying there.

The college students would see the last show of 9 to 12 and after eating two or three hot dogs, they would walk all the way to their hostel on foot. Even the day boarders, in the name of tuition, were lured by their friends into matinee show at

Jubilee and when they went late to their homes, they got scolding from their parents.

Before Jubilee came into existence, there was Rama Talkies where presently *Ramlila* was staged. In their childhood days, many people remember going to this old-fashioned talkies along with their grandfathers. Those days movies were silent. Mostly they had religious themes and many others related to wars. Romantic movies or thrillers were unknown in those times. And then time changed. Jubilee was the latest sensation of this city.

Hakim Dhari Shah was the only capable and famous doctor in the town. His medical shop was as famous as Jubilee. There were always long queues of patients at his shop from morning till nine in the night. He had employed dozens of workers. There were no multi-specialty hospitals in those days.

For the family of Hakim Dhari Shah, going to the Jubilee Cinema House used to be a very special event. Two *tongas* were hired in which the whole family along with the maids and other servants sat. Big lunch boxes in which food was packed were also kept. After watching the movie, the whole caravan would go to the company bagh, take food and picnic till late evening.

Many days before the arrival of a new movie, the officials of Jubilee Cinema, sitting in giant tongas, displaying big gaudy posters of the new film, would stride in the entire city announcing about the film as to what its cast was. They would play the songs of the film on the loudspeaker. That was the only way to make publicity those days.

In those days, a new cinema hall called Friends had also started functioning but most people of the city didn't like going there. This cinema hall was on the outer border of the city and it was not safe for a family to watch a late night show. Going there meant shelling out an extra money for rickshaw. In the matter of showing chartbuster and smash hit movies, the owners of Jubilee would outsmart Friends people since they were in this field since long and had good relations with the film distributors.

Everything was going well till Madhuri Dixit's blockbuster *Hum Aap Ke Hain Kaun*. This runaway success film ran for forty houseful weeks.

After that, countdown for the unfortunate time of Jubilee began. God forbid, such thing may not happen even to an enemy. A few weeks back, the tickets were sold in black but now, half of the seats of the hall remained unfilled.

The owners became anxious. They did new experiments. They brought some hot and sexy movies to woo the public. But it didn't make much difference.

The reason was that a new wave was flowing. Videos were becoming cheaper and Video Parlours were being opened in every tenth house which started showing latest films at cheaper rates. The market boomed with pirated CDs of films.

On national television, famous soap operas made people sit at their house in the evening. They returned home much before the start of these soap operas. They didn't want to miss any of its episode.

Before the cable network spread its roots completely, there was a faint hope of revival of good days for Jubilee. But cable TV proved fatal for it. The people whose only livelihood was to black the tickets, were running from pillar to post in search of petty jobs.

Jubilee was pulling on somehow on the strength on people from the nearby towns and villages. The college going boys and girls unfolded the unsolved knots of Vatsyayan's *Kamasutra* sitting in the dark corner seats of Jubilee. But the growing numbers of cyber café limited their entry to Jubilee now. Jubilee was on last breaths.

It is well said that rats and cowards are the first to leave a drowning ship. Ghuman Seth, the owner of Jubilee saw the slow death of Jubilee. He thought it better to go with time. He found a scapegoat. He found a gullible party and gave Jubilee to him on rental basis. The contract was signed for ten years in the first instance.

And from that day, Jubilee's slow death began. The new owner could know his foolishness only after six months. He was in a fix. He could neither leave Jubilee nor run it since the operating expenses were far more than the collections.

Near the new by-pass of the city, a brand new multiplex having a gorgeous shopping mall opened and that proved to be the final nail in the coffin of dying Jubilee. People thronged there. They had money, cars and a new lifestyle. They wanted some new thrill. Jubilee was outdated now.

It had lost all the past grandeur and majesty. Canteen was totally closed. Torn seats were not replaced for the past five years. Instead, hard ply was fixed in place of cushions. The toilets were stinking and the parking place was filthy.

No worthwhile and hit movie was screened now. Plaster of walls was falling down. Now cheap and third rate adult movies were shown here. In such vulgar shows, pirated and crude reels of sexy foreign films were showed in order to attract the rickshaw pullers, truck drivers and other drunkards and commoners. Parking for scooters and cars was closed later on since no contractor came forward because of the poor turn out.

This show of blue film would be over within one and a half hour. The police and excise authorities were given kickbacks so that they may not conduct any raid during such banned shows.

It was the final blow for Jubilee now. Recently a newspaper reported that there was a plan to bring down Jubilee Cinema. A multiplex-cum-shopping arcade was proposed to be constructed in its place. This new mall would house a hi-fi shopping centre, McDonald's restaurant, offices and other small eating joints. It was claimed that this would be the biggest multiplex in the state which would have the capacity to screen four movies at one time.

And Jubilee actually breathed its last that day. Passers-by would stop for a while when they saw two giant bulldozers and an earthmover bringing down their dear Jubilee to the ground. In the evening, old people discussed with weary heart their reminiscences and recollections about their childhood friend Jubilee.

Breaking Away

Before the advent of winter, the sky was filled with long lines of migratory birds stretching from one end to the other.

I would ask mom, "These are such colourful birds. Where do they come from, mom?"

Mom would reply, "These wise birds are the original inhabitants of cold countries situated far off. They travel thousands of miles and come to our lands because our countries are somewhat warmer. They avoid brutal snow and extreme temperatures this way. They come here for survival and in search of food. When winter is gone and good weather returns to their lands, they cross long seas and high mountains again and go back to their motherland."

Parents reply as much to their children as much as they want them to understand. That time I was an innocent kid.

Today my two sons have settled in foreign countries. Now I understand what migration is and what the pangs of separation are.

In the beginning, my kids had plans to return back after earning a good fortune. They opined that they would go and earn there but finally they would settle in their motherland. Now they have become used to living there. There is no possibility of their return. They have acquired citizenship there. Their incomes are in millions. Here they won't be able to pull on since they won't get that much pay here. Moreover their children are also studying there.

Settling in a foreign land is a very tough job. They face a sorrowful cultural shock. The relatives, who remain back also suffer. Only they know the mental agony of the parents who go through it.

Papa left his village some fifty years ago. He settled in the city where he worked. He remembered his native place all the time. Though he travelled only two hundreds miles from his birthplace but he could not forgive himself throughout his life.

He expressed through his poems this unkind pain. He depicted this cruel displacement in his writings. When I open his books and read his poems now, I understand the depth of his pathos since I also feel the same pangs and pains of separation while living away from my loved ones.

Papa would become emotional saying that sons have a heart of stone but daughter understands her parents better. She never turns her back to them. Sons follow their wives whereas a daughter never deserts her father and mother.

Mom would argue with him, "Time has changed now. There is no difference between a boy and a girl. The girl too leaves her father's house and goes to her in-laws. No one weeps for them all life. How long the parents would keep their children in their cosy protection? Even a bird does not let her baby stay for long under the warmth of her wings. As the baby gets matured, the mother kicks him out and asks him to live on his own. I fed and defended you till you were weak. Now, go and build a new world for yourself."

Papa would at once come to know that mom is just trying to console herself. Papa came two hundred miles away but my only brother, Jassi got the job in Hyderabad which was two thousands miles away.

In the beginning, mom missed him too much. She would telephone him daily. She worried about him all the time. She would narrate her dreams to me daily, just after getting up in the morning. She would weep sulkily, remembering her son.

I could not understand. My brother had a good income and even then mom was not happy. I asked her to calm down and tried to make her understand that men go to distant lands to earn. It was not a new thing. She told me that now it was a lifelong separation. Jassi would settle down there since his work was there only. And that I would know when my kids would be born.

When I got married, mom's condition worsened. But she consoled herself. As regards a daughter, it is taken for granted that she will definitely go from this house one day. For a girl, mother doesn't weep throughout her life. If the girl is well settled in her next house, parents become a happy lot. But if her son and his family go and settle far away, the mother is broken.

When Papa died, mom's heart broke completely. She was all alone now. Her grief became intolerable. Jassi had his own limitations. Mom was not ready to go to Hyderabad.

I have met the same fate today. Though I am emotionally comfortable with my husband, but my house looks desolate without kids. My children are doing well abroad but my family is incomplete without them.

I wonder whether my whole race in life was up to this point only. I had imagined living in a large family. We had constructed a triple-storey house with this idea in mind that both my sons' families would live at each floor.

Papa was upset when he was thrown two hundred miles away from his roots and mom was depressed when her son was displaced two thousands miles. They had one common thing. These people remained within the country.

Nature was very cruel to me. She threw my sons more than ten thousand miles away. To go to them, I have to fly over many an unknown country.

It doesn't seem that they too are happy there. They went through a big mental and cultural shock — new land, new culture, new language. Even foreign plants refuse to grow elsewhere though they do not possess finer sensibilities like we human beings.

In my childhood days, when she would see long lines of migratory birds in the month of December, mom would say to me one more thing, "My dear Bubbly, the migratory birds are saner and wiser than we people. They come here and at the end of the severe winter, go back to their own country. They love their country."

I look around and wonder about the latest trend everywhere. Sending children abroad for study and job has become a new fashion these days. There is a great rush at the passport and visa offices. The window of visa office opens at nine in the morning but people line up before the window from the midnight.

It is truly said that grass is always greener on the other side of the fence. The craze for going abroad and settling in foreign lands would increase so much, no one had imagined. Now no one likes an Indian salary. The glitter of pounds and dollars allures everybody.

Mom had reconciled with the circumstances. She had forgotten about the pangs of separation of her son. When she visited me, she returned relieved and comforted.

She lives in a small town. There is simplicity in relationships, lifestyle, attitudes and way of thinking in her town. People feel and show a sense of belonging to each other.

When she comes to meet me in this metropolitan city, she usually says, "Bubbly beta, now I don't remember Jassi that much. I talk to you on phone and become sure that one of my children is near me."

Wiping her tears she would say, "Now I have grown old. It is becoming difficult for me to reach to your house here. The identification marks which I had marked last year for reaching here, have all changed so much. The map and contours of your city is changing very speedily. New malls and big multiplexes are erected everywhere and the old buildings are being pulled down. Now for an elderly and aged person like me, it is becoming increasingly difficult to cross these hectic roads and reach your house. You should come to me after every six months and stay with me for a week."

Suddenly her tone changes, "I wonder how you live here. Everyone remains reserved and shut inside the house. In our town, I have friendships with a score of ladies; they come and sit in my house frequently. I go to them. We have dozens of social activities. Times passes very easily and happily. Don't you feel bored and sluggish watching television all the day? Your husband remains busy at Stock Exchange. There is so much hubbub, rush and commotion all around. Your city is becoming hell day by day."

When the night falls, the mountains of fears and suspicions look darker to us. I and mom start discussing the tales of memories and separations of ours dear ones. My condition has also become similar to that of mom. She visits her son at Chennai and stays there for a month or so. All goes well but then she feels drawn to her place where she spent seventy years of her life and she returns back. She feels she can't stay there for good.

We too went abroad three times to live with our sons, daughters-in-law and grandchildren. There seemed no possibility that we would be able to cope up with them and pass the rest of our lives with ease or compose.

Moreover they also didn't press us hard to stay with them. The value system and lifestyle is different there. We can't match with that fast pace and their way of life. We have roots fixed here. A sapling can be planted anywhere but a giant tree if uprooted can't go well elsewhere.

Mom would say, "In my town, we have a large number of oldies living alone. Their children don't come for years together. All the best and able young men have migrated to foreign lands. Only frail, old, ill and seriously sick persons are left."

With moist eyes she narrates, "People from the eastern Uttar Pradesh have taken over the job of agriculture and animal rearing. There is prosperity all around. Dollars are pouring but the zest in life is gone. On the surface, it looks all calm and composed. Life goes on. All works are completed, but there is a listlessness and dullness in life. There seems a great pomp and show in social functions and marriages but that gusto and passionate delight is missing. Can they eat dollars? In this old age, they wear costly silk and hang weighty diamonds and roam in luxury cars. It is not a soothing thing. The heart is emotionally frail and blank. There is grimness like death all over. In our heart of heart, we all yearn to play with our grandchildren."

Mom would burst into tears. I too, couldn't control myself. We lessen our grief, washing it away with tears.

It looks our neighbours are happy. They say, "Look, in India, a boy may get a degree but gets no good job. The world has shrunk now. It has become a global village. We can go anywhere within no time. What is important is that there should be money in our pocket. Moreover, we spend millions on the education of our children. Will all of them get jobs in their city only? They will go to Gurgaon, Bangalore or Canada. There is hardly any difference. They become self-sufficient. Then; where is the problem?"

Talking about the real problem, their tongue trembles. Their voice becomes heavy. Tears flow from their eyes.

But what can they do? Before a third person, they conceal their grief and sorrow. When they are all alone, they weep bitterly. When they meet and associate with a likeminded person, their anguish and torment burst out.

When I share my sorrow with mom or a close friend, I feel relieved and comforted. No universal remedy has been discovered for these pangs of separation.

Mom still says what she used to say earlier, "Bubbly dear, these migratory birds are thousand times better than human beings. These birds always return to their original homes.

The human race is very selfish and self-seeking. Where it finds affluence and prosperity, it settles down there unmindful of the fact that those whom they have left, how will they live without them?"

Mom is over ninety now. When she sees the migratory birds returning back, she goes indoors and sobs silently. I too go into a deep sea of thoughts — no solutions, no answers to these painful separations. We wished our sons to conquer the world. Now they did. We should be happy.

A Happy Ending

This was his second unlucky day today. Kisna was standing outside the huge, black iron gate of Mr. Mehta again. His face was grim and gloomy. In his heart, there was a growing resentment as to why he took birth in a lower caste.

The gate was tightly closed. From a small crack, Kisna could make out every now and then what was going on inside the house of his employer. He was fired from his job. He was working at the farmhouse of Mr. Mehta. In the recent elections, the representatives of lower caste had won. The stalwarts of upper castes could not digest it. They retaliated.

Just a few moments ago he had seen Mr. Mehta coming towards the gate. His heart started thumping heavily thinking that Mr. Mehta was about to call him in but he turned towards his drawing room. Kisna was disappointed.

His impatience grew but how could he face his master who was not ready to employ him? He thought how long he should wait for a call from inside. He should himself go and resolve the matter of discord between him and Mr. Mehta. But he could not dare.

Yesterday he saw Mr. Mehta in a very angry mood. He was shouting at his wife at a high pitch. Kisna stood the whole day outside the gate in the hope of being summoned in.

His legs were weary and completely tired at the end of the day. There was a severe cold. Just a few yards from him he could see dancing children who had made a bonfire. Kisna too wanted to go and warm himself but he positioned himself outside the gate lest Mr. Mehta call him to resume duty.

He was expelled from his job a month ago. After the current village elections when Mr. Mehta lost his grip over the village, he was so infuriated that he fired his low-caste servant. All the upper caste stalwarts took the same step.

Kisna knew that Mr. Mehta was a hot-tempered person but still he knew his real nature. He was otherwise a kind-hearted person and quite compassionate to his servants. He knew the real worth of a dutiful and compliant man but this time the stars of Kisna had put him in this trouble.

Last year when Kisna left Mr. Mehta and joined Dalip's farm, Mr. Mehta had become very angry with him. He came personally to his thatched hut and with fire in his eyes lashed him with these words, "We fed you for generations and for a few more bucks and a verbal thrashing from me, you have joined Dalip Singh, my rival. You didn't have any regard for me." He also cursed Kisna's mother. The very next day Kisna came back to Mehta's farm.

Kisna was just 14 when he became the bonded labourer of Mr. Mehta. Before Kisna, his father held that position. His father remained 24 hours at the agricultural farm of Mr. Mehta.

If Kisna or his mother were to seek any advice from him, they had to go to him personally in the fields. The bare necessities of daily life were provided from Mr. Mehta's house.

And on that dreadful night when Kisna's father died from snake's bite, Kisna took his father's place. He was not that loyal and submissive as was his father. At times he would behave like a child and would run away from the farm for weeks. Mr. Mehta would keep him again after abusing and scolding him.

Last year Kisna absented himself for more than a month. Mr. Mehta sent him many messages. Kisna was allured by his father-in-law who had promised him a good job in a factory in a nearby town. He worked there but found that job too tedious and tiring. At Mehta's farm there was not much work for Kisna. But this job demanded tending and caring for the cattle round the clock.

Now this present chaos was created by the Kisna's clan in the elections for village chief. Mehta and other upper caste members were thrown out of power this time and their places were filled by lower caste people who had been denied representation in village body for centuries. Kisna thought differently.

The wretched position in which he was finding himself today was due to Beeru Pradhan of his caste who defeated Mr. Mehta with a very narrow margin. Mr. Mehta was under this impression that his own servant and his family voted against him.

That's why Parsa, the representative of Blacksmith kinfolk told Beeru Pradhan clearly, "This politics does not suit us. We are a labour class. We have to earn our daily bread.

We supported you and now these upper caste landlords have boycotted us and our families are suffering. We are compelled to borrow at higher interest rates to feed ourselves."

It was a long time today that Kisna kept standing outside Mr. Mehta's house. He was totally fatigued. He was ready to swear that in reality he had voted in favour of his master.

Nobody was there to believe him. The entire village had become his enemy. Beeru Pradhan had given him a thousand rupees after the elections to tide over the situation but that too had been exhausted. The shopkeepers had refused to give him grocery on credit.

For not a single day he was employed by the contractor, cold storage or other farmhouses since the upper caste people had decided not to employ lower caste labourers. They wanted to smash their poise.

Now Kisna saw through a small fissure of the gate that Mr. Mehta was packing his luggage to go to Delhi to meet his son. "He may take a month to come back to the village," thought Kisna.

By that time Kisna and his family would totally starve. If he won't dare to talk to Mr. Mehta now and then, he would be ruined totally.

Kisna opened the gate with trembling hands. He stood before Mr. Mehta with his eyes fixed on the ground. Mr. Mehta was on the sofa smoking his cigar. For a few moments no one spoke.

Kisna summoned courage and spoke in a humble voice, "Master, I swear by God that in the elections, our family voted for you." He bowed down and touched the ground in testimony of his truth.

Mr. Mehta burst into laughter on hearing this. He knew Kisna's real worth. No one could be his equal in manual work. When Kisna remained at his farm there was no worry about the cattle.

He laughed at the innocence of Kisna. He spoke, "Kisna, how could I win with your single vote? This time your whole clan rose against me. I never had a taste of defeat for the past 50 years. When I lost the elections I went mad and sent a message to lower caste person like you not to come to work in my farm but leave it. What a stupid person like you have to do with the village politics. I realised in a week that we are incomplete without your support. I was eagerly waiting for your return. Okay, get on the job right now. I am going to Delhi. Take special care of that pregnant jersey cow…."

Kisna's joys knew no bounds. He forgot his humiliation, his tiredness, his hunger and his bitterness. He ran at once towards the farmhouse. He was in a fix to decide as to which job he should attend first.

Mr. Mehta fastened the laces of his shoes. He said to his wife in a triumphant voice, "Look dear, how I turned the events in my favour! We can do without these people, but they are finished if we are displeased with them."

Point Blank

Manohar would start narrating the same boring story of his known people whenever he met me.

Last week when he met me near the elevator and gave this information, "Do you remember that Mohan Lal? He has become an inspector in excise and customs department. He is reeling in millions these days. He would have been a Major in the army today but it was his ill-luck that his result was torn by his naughty nephews. Later on he was recruited as a soldier and then after getting voluntary retirement he took the benefit of ex-serviceman and was selected as an inspector in excise and customs. These days he is posted in Mumbai."

I had just joined his department as an officer. We had no contact with each other for more than past twenty years. He belonged to my native village. His elder brother was my class fellow up to 10th standard. Then our family moved to numerous cities since my father was in armed services.

Whenever I asked about him, he would start telling me other people's tales. He remembered even the minute details about them. I had forgotten the names, professions and other whereabouts of people of my village since I was posted in numerous cities in different civil departments.

Manohar would get hold of me whenever he met me in the corridors of office, conference hall or in the market. With great interest and taking full liberty of our previous common connections at village level, he would draw the life sketch and narrate the life history of anyone as if he was narrating it for the first time.

He would forget that he had told me the same story just a few days back. He didn't hesitate even if some other officer was with me.

His knowledge about his people was quite up-to-date. He had full details of where his known person was posted, what his post was, what salary he got, how many kids he had and in which classes they were, when and with whom he was married etc. All these petite details were always on his tips.

He remembered each incident and the date and year of its happening, and with great passion and interest he would unfold these tales repeatedly to me. He would relate these details as if he had crammed them.

It was impossible to avoid Manohar. Though we sat in different buildings he had made his routine to meet me at least once a week to unload all that humbug into my unenthusiastic ears.

I had been forgetting the names of my childhood friends and class fellows. Now ever since I had met Manohar I had started recollecting the chain of events and unforgettable part of my childhood memories since Manohar was repeatedly revising these anecdotes daily.

Initially I was irritated by this weird nature of Manohar. My fellow officers usually commented, "This clerk Manohar Lal is a very strange fellow. He gives you the boring news and unnecessary details of forlorn people like a tape recorder. I think the screws of his brain are loose."

I used to say in light tone, "His screws are not only loose but I think they are not there in their proper place. Well, he is from my village. We had disposed the property there after the death of parents. Now it is this Manohar who keeps me informed about the people there. Strange as he is, maybe a psychologically ill person, I don't like his nonsense but I sometimes relish his baloney. I know about his inferiority complex. His brothers are all well placed. He has lagged behind in his life. Now it is his only interest to match himself with them by updating details about his kinsfolk. He feels proud that he knows so many successful people."

I narrated Manohar's strange and whimsical tales to my wife and she also started liking him. She became interested in his family.

One day she proposed, "Look, he seems such a nice person and belongs to your native place. Your post is transferable. After four years you will be posted somewhere else. Let us visit him some day. It will be a great fun."

I could hardly tolerate him in the office. I shuddered at the thought of family level contacts. It would be unbearable for me to digest his stupid tales.

To discourage my wife I took a defensive stand and said, "Well, we should be careful, he is just a clerk in my office. I won't relish if you raised any fury at his house or made him a butt of ridicule in front of other officers' wives."

But my wife would have none of it. Manohar was thrilled when we visited him one Sunday morning. He welcomed us with great enthusiasm.

After a few formal talks he started his pointless stories, "Do you remember that Gopal, the only son of Mr. Kaushal, who had broken his arm while playing in childhood? Arre! That black boy who was the class fellow of your elder brother! He is the Superintendent of Police Jails these days and is posted in our city. I met him only the day before yesterday. I sat in his grand office for one hour. What a big office, sir, more than double your room! Gopal is very simple and friendly. He called his P.A. and told him frankly not to send anyone while I was sitting with him. He ordered *jalebis*, pastries and *rasgoolas*. We chatted for two hours. He was married in a top class businessmen family of Mumbai. His wife is also a Class One officer. She is related to the wife of the brother-in-law of my elder brother. And that fellow Kashmiri Shah of our village, he is a famous contractor in the city."

My wife quite liked his tales. I had had enough of all this trash many times before, so I found an excuse and leaving my wife and children there, I set out for an urgent work.

Manohar started coming to our house regularly now. His wife was of reserved nature. My wife liked her too. She was a teacher in a school. Since both Manohar and his wife were working, they had maintained a good standard of their house. Their kids were smart and intelligent.

Manohar started coming to my cabin more often. Now his tales were becoming more frank, open and daring. He would share every secret with me.

Though I felt bored and choked, I didn't felt like stopping him from talking lest he should mind it. He started criticising other officers, their high-handedness, their corrupt practices and their mean ways to outsmart each other.

He started accompanying me to the office functions and market places. In the beginning, he felt restrained and hesitated in the company of my fellow officers.

Whenever he found me a bit alone he never missed the chance to narrate his oft repeated tales of some of our common acquaintance. He felt comforted and relieved after telling his story.

Manohar was remorseful to have remained a clerk throughout his life while most of his class fellows were officers now.

Quite often he reacted bitterly, "Sir, you were promoted at the right time. I am doomed to rot here. The departmental examinations have been scrapped now otherwise I would have become a sectional head by now. Well, no matter, I and my wife both earn more than thirty thousands in a month. We live in a majestic way; you have seen our *kothi* and our standard. I have seen many class-one officers of this office who ride on scooters. We have a car for the past ten years. My kids are in the convent schools. With great sweat, I got them admitted there. The brother-in-law of Sampat, my wife's cousin, is District Education Officer here. I went to him for a recommendation letter and he telephoned the Principal and my son got the admission, though there were no seats available and again at the time of admission of my girl…"

I already knew all those stories very well so I diverted his attention to other official matters for a relief.

There also Manohar blurted out his frustration, "Sir, this office squeezes we people totally. It pays fifteen thousand bucks but extracts worth fifty thousands from us. By God when we reach home in the evening, we are totally exhausted and drained out. One has to pay a great cost if one's wife is a working lady. Right in the morning all the four members of my family are on the roads."

Mahohar was fuming and fretting. His face became red with rage and his body started trembling and his lips were fluttering. With much effort he could be cooled down.

Manohar did not have that good reputation in the office. He would easily irritate his seniors. Everyone had serious grouses against him.

When he started associating with me, he started ignoring the work on his seat completely. Maybe he was in this impression that I would shield him.

One or two officers complained to me regarding his work and conduct, "What has happened to this LDC Manohar Lal. He is not at all bothered about the work at his seat. The other day he challenged Mr. Tiwari. You know that Mr. Tiwari is a very strict and demanding officer with regard to punctuality and official work. Now you should advise Manohar. He is from your village. His career can be spoiled. His pay for the last month has been withheld because he was absent from the office. He didn't bother to get his leave sanctioned even after a month. You know how tough the big boss is. He will hang him if he doesn't mend his ways."

I asked Manohar about this fuss. He was quite angry, "Sir, I am doing the work of two seats. This is a strange convention of this office. A person working as a silent ass gets more work but the man who challenges these corrupt officers makes merry without doing any work. You know that Chhedi Lal, roaming free like an ox, always ready to abuse if some officer teased him unnecessarily. I was on leave for a week. I sent application from my house. Mr. Tiwari raised the whole office on his head. I give a damn to him. I sacrificed my whole life for the office and still remained a clerk. Not even a single promotion was given to me. They can't demote me as a peon, then why should I bother?"

I comforted Manohar, "Look, the rules of the office are very strict. The new big boss doesn't spare anyone. I being in All India cadre can be transferred anytime. Don't flout rules. I have phoned Mr. Tiwari. You go and say sorry to him and in future be watchful of your job. It is difficult to get a good job these days. Don't squander it."

Manohar didn't compromise. He openly challenged everyone. Later on I heard that he slapped the officer in-charge.

The officers took a tough stand and charge sheeted him. After a month he was suspended.

Apprehending that he was unnecessarily dragging me in his case, I took a three month leave and went to Goa on a vacation.

When I came back, I heard that Manohar's entry to the office was banned because of more cases of his misbehaviour.

I talked to my fellow officers and they took a lenient view but Manohar was nowhere to be seen. He became underground for six months. The people of the office hunted for him. Letters addressed to him returned undelivered.

One odd day he came to my residence. He was a different Manohar now. He had grown a full beard. He was wearing rough jeans. He had a bundle of readymade clothes with him. My wife prepared tea for him. I was expecting some old tale of Mohan, Sampat or Devidayal.

He was telling about his new line of business in sombre tone, "Sir, there is a good season of woollens this time. I have specially brought for you some pullovers. I will give you at factory rate. I have taken the agency of branded sports shoes. I have constructed two floors my *kothi* and I am getting ten thousand rent per month. I am planning to…"

I was filled with a strange feeling that is this same Manohar who was always full of talks about other people, their professions, their achievements and never mentioning about himself? Now a minor shock from the office has made him more down-to-earth and realistic. He once lived in a world of dreams but he is talking sense now.

I was about to tell him that I have tried to get his case cleared but I stopped myself. Thinking that on getting the news of his suspension case resolved, he may not become the same crazy Manohar and start telling me about his village fellows and their relatives, I reserved myself. I started choosing pullovers from the stock of woollens brought by him.

Second Innings

Today a unique competition was being organised in the auditorium of Bravo Old-Age Home. Every year on 30th June and 31st December, a special function was held in this renowned old-age home in the capital city of India.

The reputation of this home was widely spread. It was a fact that an amount of Rupees Fifty Thousand was required to be deposited as booking amount in order to get membership of this prestigious old-age home.

The popularity of this home was evident from the fact that when Class One officer bring Bravo Home's membership form to his house, his proud and disobedient children were scared because of social stigma lest their parents may join this old-age home.

Today's prestigious session of Bravo Home was very special in the sense that all the dignitaries of the mega city were present to attend the function.

Entries from men and women living in this home for the past three years were invited. Five people were chosen out of them who were called upon the stage to tell the select gathering about the changes in their lifestyles, attitudes and quality of life after having joined the Bravo Home. These real life stories showed positive changes and satisfaction drawn by the occupants of this home.

The chairman of the Bravo Home, in his sweet and impressive voice declared, "His Majesty, General B.S. Pradhan, Governor, Punjab and Chandigarh, Honourable Justice P.K. Sahni, Shree Raman Jindal, Member of Parliament, distinguished guests, and ladies and gentlemen, I welcome all of you to a very special eventful evening at Bravo Old-Age Home. There has been a potential rise in the popularity of our Bravo Home. For me, this is not a healthy sign of a good society. In the last phase of his life, a person can enjoy the fruits of lifelong struggle only at his very own house.

"Anyway, in our city alone, more than a dozen old-age homes are working successfully. 99% of these homes are working with the sole motto of earning maximum profit at the cost of life. We know that quality of life and other facilities provided there are below the mark. We know these facts from the stories of neglect and exploitation narrated by our old friends joining our home after getting poor services at other homes.

"These unlucky fellows tell us how they were humiliated after joining those homes. The pain and suffering in these old-age homes was much more than the insult and neglect shown by their own children.

"By the way, Bravo Home has evolved a unique system of life for the retired and ageing persons. After joining this home, we have noticed positive and remarkable changes in their lives and some of them won laurels in many walks of life viz. social service, awareness and spreading literacy after getting inspired by their stay in the home.

"One of our inmates, Mr. Vijaymohan Gupta has been awarded *Padma shree* by the Honourable President of India in the field of social service and our another member Justice Prem Singh has got President's medal for his outstanding service to the welfare of lepers. How much can I mention? The list is very long. You people must be reading in the newspapers and magazines about the achievements of the members of this home.

"Ladies and gentlemen, and now I am coming to that interesting part of the event for which we all have assembled here. As per our six-monthly routine, we have made our efforts to present before you a team of five speakers who were selected by our honourable jury from sixty entries.

"As per our rules, the best of the today's speakers will win a 3-months world tour package. The selection will be made by our Honourable Governor, Justice Sahni and Mr. Jindal, M.P., Chandigarh.

"Now I invite the participants and request them to present their resumes in the alphabetical order of their names. They will themselves give their introductions and will share their rich and heartfelt experiences with all of us. Wishing them the best of luck, I take my seat. Thank you once again for giving me a patient hearing."

The first speaker told his story, "I am A.P. Chauhan. I retired as a Principal from the Government College. I am a part of this home for the last seven years. After my wife's death, I sold my 2-kanal house and joined this home. It was not that I had any difficulty in my own house but after my wife's death, an incident brought me here. I was enjoying a decent life and my health was excellent. My son was well-settled. I was fond of reading books, so passing time was no problem for a person like me."

"After the sudden demise of my wife, I could not control myself. My friends came to my help but they took advantage of my loneliness. I was getting a handsome pension. I took to drinking in the company of my friends. There was no one to check me now.

"My fun-loving bohemian friends took me to Simla, Goa and Kathmandu. For the first time, I felt the thrill in my life. I acquired the membership of all the three premier clubs in the capital. I started going there daily, enjoying chess, rummy and cocktail parties.

"I forgot the cruel separation of my wife. I had made a nice bar in my room too. Sometimes when my son and his family would visit me, I felt restrained. When they would go, we friends became happy again.

"And then the inevitable happened. I was paralysed. I spent money like water but I remained confined to the wheelchair. My fair-weather friends disappeared one by one since I was of no use to them now.

"My own son expressed his inability to take me along with him. My servant took me for a stroll putting me in my wheelchair. The whole colour of the life was gone. Then I thought of God. I sold my house and came to this home. The home gave me so much love and affection that I became a normal person once again.

"I spent seven years here. I came to know the real utility of a family life. I devoted my time to do a P.G. degree in Psychology. I started a helpline for the destitute and infirm.

"Along with a circle of friends here, I started new concepts of healthy life like yoga, laughter and clapping therapy in the adjoining parks. We held seminars on generation gap, AIDS and inter-family interactions.

"We emphasised on the fact that if all aged persons would throng the old-age homes, then the very existence of family institution would be endangered. I repeat painfully that though Bravo Home is an ideal place to stay, yet our very own dwelling unit is our real sweet home.

"I sincerely feel that elderly people should live gracefully in their own homes. Let us reserve the old-age homes only for the real needy and lonely persons. I see how youngsters of affluent families heave a sigh of relief after sending their oldies to Bravo Home.

"This is a very dangerous trend. Please help us arrest this unhealthy inclination otherwise the very existence of mankind would be eliminated. Thank you."

The second speaker came on the stage and told her tale, "Ladies and gentlemen, my name is Bimla Agnihotri. I was working as a Manager in a bank. Ten years ago, I was married to an NRI. After three long years of humiliation, my divorce case was finalised. I tell you the reasons."

"My husband was already married abroad. I went to the court. It took me three painful years to get out of that sweltering hell. During this period, I got bitter experiences of my life.

"Everybody looked at me with explicit motives of selfishness and lust, be it my boss or my landlord or my advocate. I got five million bucks as compensation from my husband and all sundry was at my feet.

"Many handsome young men, who were half my age, were ready to marry me, not out of love but for my money. I was sick of all that nonsense. One day, I read about this home in the newspaper. I took voluntary retirement from my job and came here.

"I said to myself — if I had to face litigation for three long years to get freedom from a fraudulent marriage in this male-dominated society, what must be the plight of those unlucky women who had neither money nor proper guidance?

"After coming to the Bravo Home, I started a lifeline for those needy persons who had been denied their lawful right.

"Many lawyers have joined me since then and we were successful in providing justice in more than hundred cases…"

The story stayed there for long. The audience patiently listened to all the speakers. In every story, it sensed double standards of human nature and a sharp decline in the warmth and sincerity in human relationships.

After the story session of five contestants, there started an unending chain of boring and mind-numbing speeches of politicians and bureaucrats and it became unbearable for the story to stand that verbal bombast. It sneaked out of that hall in a flash of time.

A Perfect Butcher

Mr. Mehra was a very shrewd man but with no principles. The whole office was familiar with his impious ways. He was an officer with no officer-like qualities. Apart from expecting kickback from his subordinates, he never missed a chance to wring anyone else who wanted to get some favour from him. The other day Trilochan was narrating his appalling tale.

Trilochan spoke in a defeated tone, "Adulation was clearly evident in the words of Mr. Mehra." He paused for a moment, and clearing his throat he continued, "The story relates to the time when I was a clerk but I was not under the charge of Mr. Mehra. One day when I was passing outside the cabin of Mr. Mehra, he called me to listen to him for a moment. I realised then and there that I was going to be in trouble. He would either demand some money or would ask me to do an odd job. Gathering some courage, I stepped in. Mr. Mehra was revolving his ashtray with one hand and holding mobile in another. In an impressive voice he spoke, 'Yes, Mr. Trilochan, in which section are you posted these days?' In heart of heart I was feeling amused as Mr. Mehra knew the name of a petty clerk like me, but the moment I became conscious of any possible trap laid by him, I alerted myself."

Trilochan went on, "Mr. Mehra lit a cigarette and offered one to me. But how could I smoke before an officer? He took a deep puff and said, 'How is your son who was in Army School, where is he now?' I could not believe he was taking interest in my domestic affairs. I became more cautious. I had listened to numerous tales of Mr. Mehra, the way he coaxed his subordinates in one way or the other and then emptied their pockets. I replied briefly and dryly. After a brief gossip about the office affairs, moving swiftly towards his cupboard in his revolving chair, he took out a sort of collection notebook from his drawer and placed it on the table right before me. Now he straightened his posture and revolving the paper weight with full force and then catching it, he took a deep puff from his cigarette. Then he spoke in a pleasant voice, 'Mr. Trilochan, you know, normally I don't involve myself much with these trivial religious affairs. I am a real devotee Lord Shiva. The priests of our temple are setting up a huge *lingam* this *Shivratri* and they approached me saying that being a big officer I should contribute significantly in this noble cause. Now once I assumed responsibility I must trouble god-fearing and religious people like you'."

Trilochan said with a heavy heart, "I could not say no in the name of religion. I had to pay five hundred bucks then and there. Mr. Mehra is impossible. You can't escape his trap. If he has set his eyes on you, you are in his web. He listens to no excuses; rather his plan of robbing you is always unique.

You know that you are being befooled but even then you are duped."

The case of Mr. Gopal, senior accountant was a bit different. It was very pitiable. Mr. Mehra called him to his cabin a week after he joined the section under his direct charge.

Mr. Gopal stated his story, "I was quite mentally prepared for the token money that my boss expected from me but the amount would be so high I had not dreamt of. Mr. Mehra said to me, 'Look Mr. Gopal, you are on public dealing seat and have joined this fertile section for the first time; you have to share your booty with me. I set the amount as Rupees Five Thousands per month. Thereafter no one will disturb you.' I took the risk and paid him the sum the next day. But after a week he gave me his electricity bill saying that he forgot his cheque book at home. Being the last date of the bill that day, somehow I paid the bill."

Mr. Gopal said with heavy heart, "But there is a limit of squeezing an accountant. These days the public has become very aware. You can't ask much for a petty case. Mounting demands from Mr. Mehra compelled me to ask for bribes from everybody getting work done from me. I didn't spare even my fellow workers. Now everyone is not in hurry or willing to pay bribe but I would hook everyone by delaying the work on one pretext or the other. I thought Mr. Mehra would save me from every possible danger. Someone reported my mean methods to the vigilance wing and one bad morning I was caught in their net red-handedly taking bribe money. I came to know later on that Mr. Mehra knew about all this. He had good relations with the vigilance staff but he didn't forewarn me. Then a charge sheet was framed against me and Mr. Mehra bargained with me for fifty thousands rupees to hush up the whole matter. Such are his ways of pillaging his own office people. Seeing his crooked ways even devil would feel ashamed."

Mrs. Neena's story also portrayed the wicked image of Mr. Mehra. She was posted in the office on compassionate grounds after the sudden demise of her husband. She was getting full pension of her husband. Now as per latest government's orders one couldn't get dearness allowance on salary as well on pension. Mr. Mehra managed to get this information from someone that Mrs. Neena draws dearness allowance on pay and pension both. He called her to his cabin and threatened her that she could be expelled from the job because she had concealed such an important fact and cheated the government to the tune of Rupees Twenty Thousand. Mr. Mehra also tried to bring her into his fold so that he could exploit her sexually but Neena was not lured. Whatever he demanded, she paid him in cash and got her case cleared.

Mr. Mehra spared no one, not even his peon. Whosoever talked of him had a pathetic tale to narrate. One day nature took her toll. Mr. Mehra was retuning from a marriage party in his car. In the wee hours of early morning, his car was run over by a speeding truck. The driver of the car and Mr. Mehra's only son sitting on the front seat were killed. Mr. Mehra and his wife were seriously injured. In the funeral ground, Mr. Mehra was brought in a wheel chair with bandages on legs and arms. He was pale and languid. The whole office was gathered there. Everyone was cursing Mr. Mehra that he earned curses of scores of people and nature had done some justice now.

A month later, Mr. Mehra resumed his official duties. For a month, he was quite kind and considerate, but then he came in his real array. One day Trilochan was talking to Gopal Babu about Mr. Mehra that there had been a sea change in Mr. Mehra. But Gopal said, “No way sir, big thugs and mean thieves never mend their ways. After the death of his only son, Mr. Mehra has become crueller. He has become a total savage, not fearful of God at all. Previously he was a bit scared of the wrath of God but now he is as cruel as devil. He has lost his only son, and so has nothing to lose. Only God will save us now.”

Bohemian

"A man smart enough can do justice at more than two levels," Mr. Taneja's eyes gleamed as he said these words.

Lighting a cigarette, he threw his next verbal bombast, "The last puff of a cigarette and the first kiss of a woman are always superb. It takes a week to know a town completely but you can peep through a woman's heart in just one night."

Mr. Taneja grasped my hand, examined it closely keeping it at different angles, took out his pen and drew out a few odd lines here and a few points there at various mounts of my hand.

He chuckled a bit and remarked, "In your affairs with girls you are a total failure, a novice indeed. You get embittered every time."

I unleashed my pent-up feelings, "In my case, the beginning is always good and response from the other side is quick but after a few weeks the girl becomes indifferent and cold. What is in my heart doesn't come to my lips. See if there is any line of love or romance."

I became curious to know about my love life.

Mr. Taneja lit another cigarette. Throwing aside my hand, he spoke in a philosopher's tone, "Have you ever seen a spider and her web? You will notice that her web has holes of different sizes and shapes. Who knows of which size and shape an insect would get trapped in her web? As soon as any prey gets stuck in her web, the spider doesn't pounce on it in haste; she waits calmly for a few moments. The poor prey flutters for his life for some seconds and then gives up every hope of survival. Only then the spider comes forward and devours it. In a similar way, you shouldn't be over-conscious about the presence of women around you. When womenfolk get this feeling that this man is out and out after them, they start ignoring him."

Mr. Taneja took a deep puff and kept on sermonising, "Moreover it is not wise to exhaust your whole energy solely on one woman. You must know about the Ludo game. Take out all the counters and keep them pushing slowly one by one. Push the one quickly which is near its home and keep the others at safe points. There are certain safe places where you can place the counters for as long as you wish. In the same way, open different fronts with different promising ladies having potentials, try winning them, who knows which one easily gives up and become your beloved."

Mr. Taneja continued, "Women are like shadows. You can't just have them by simply hankering after them madly. Instead they abhor people that follow them without speaking about their real purpose. Be frank with them but don't let them judge your inner sinister designs. Keep meeting them, continue pouring your favours on them but it should not be misunderstood by them that all this is a specially designed ambush and you are madly after them. The message should go that it is all a chance and that both of you are coming across each other frequently as a matter of coincidence."

Taking a sip of water Mr. Taneja said, "Can you tell me why man commands a superior position in the society as compared to his better half? I tell you the real reason. He is cunning. He praises the brains of a beautiful woman which she rarely possesses. Moreover while praising the beauty of an ugly woman, he employs all the marvellous similes and superb metaphors. It is an amazing tact. It pays greatly to praise a quality that doesn't exit at all, especially in case of a gorgeous and attractive woman."

I became wonderstruck at the extraordinary brilliance of Mr. Taneja. He carried on further, "It is an art to praise a woman. It is a technique which can be learnt from a love guru, an expert in these matters. In America there are skilled professionals who teach you how to flirt with women successfully. I myself took such magnificent trainings thrice. Remember one thing — you should have a clear concept in your mind as to why you need the company of a specific woman at a particular time. Praising a girl as regards her talent or beauty is a skill. Talking about beauty or her qualities directly on her face is a plain statement any amateur will make. It should look like a compliment specially drafted for her. It should be told to her in a heartfelt way looking straight into her eyes. It is stupid to go to a woman solely for sex. You can procure it elsewhere cheaper. I myself buy a call girl frequently. There are no hassles involved in it. You should think differently for the girl you want for a long-term relationship. Once you succeed to win her emotionally then everything will be yours."

Mr. Taneja had met us just six months back. It was my routine to take coffee along with my friend daily at the Grand Café.

One day, it was a great rush there. Due to New Year's celebrations there was a big crowd in the market. The café was horribly packed. Mr. Taneja couldn't get a seat anywhere. He came to our table and asked, "Young men! Can I share the table with you?"

We agreed gladly. Mr. Taneja looked quite strange on that day, with an odd pony tail, and a bundle of newspapers and magazines tucked in his armpit. But his American accent was fabulous and impressive.

He lit a cigarette and offered us too. Since we didn't smoke, we ordered a coffee for him. Puffing carelessly he said, "Yes surely I will take coffee. By the way, I am Mr. Taneja."

We also introduced ourselves to him.

Mr. Taneja told about himself in detail, "I had immigrated to the United States in early seventies. My sister was already settled there. I had lost my parents in my early childhood. I was a promising Chartered Accountant. My sister arranged my job in the States. I left my job in India. Those days my salary here was just one thousand bucks but in USA my weekly pay was three times than that. Soon I was married to a French girl there but our marriage lasted for just five years. I had two daughters from my marriage. My wife is married again but I swore not to be emotionally entwined with her again. She is still one of my best friends."

Mr. Taneja met us daily in the café. He told us interesting things about America and its society.

One day he said, "My elder daughter Rita will turn sixteen next month. I will have to go there. When a kid is sixteen there, they hold a big celebration. There is a big dissimilarity in the cultures of Indian and American societies. In India, womenfolk have a thousand reservations and inhibitions. Even a woman above forty doesn't dare to move from one city to another, but there is much liberty and freedom available to American women. My younger daughter was just twelve when she went to France all alone. I myself like to travel alone. In our flights, we make real friends – male or female – it doesn't matter. We value such relationships. Traditional Indian families are rare to be found there. When a child is sixteen, the parents stop spending on him. The whole system is different there — self-dependence and liberty are the ruling principles of life. Nobody wants to be a burden on anyone. A lot of sponsors and scholarships are available all around. India will take a century to reach that stage."

One day Mr. Taneja remarked, "Can you tell my age? I am fifty-five but look like a forty-year-old guy. In India, a person after forty finds himself heading towards temple. In West, true life begins after forty. Women start taking serious notice in you. But everything there is transitory as if on makeshift basis. Nothing is permanent. Women come in and go out of your life frequently. An emotional person can't pull on happily there. That is why I get fed up there very soon. Every year I come to India and stay here for six months. There is my native village near Moga but mostly I stay in a hotel in Chandigarh. I keep roaming at numerous religious places. I like Haridwar very much. People from all corners of India come to offer prayers for their dead relatives, but those cold-blooded priests rob them. They look exactly like American businessmen."

For two weeks, Mr. Taneja didn't turn up to the café. We thought that he had gone to USA without informing us. One early morning we found him already sitting there when we stepped into the café. A pretty and nice-looking woman in her late thirties was also sitting with him.

Pointing towards the woman, he said, "I won a grand lottery this time. Every year I come to India in search of a good wife. My daughters press me to bring an Indian bride every time I fly towards East. This time I was lucky to meet Poonam. Only this Sunday we got married. We are leaving for America next week. You know about the sweet sixteen celebration of my elder daughtcr. My daughters will be greatly thrilled to get their new mom. A single parent doesn't command much respect there. I wanted to invite both of you in my modest marriage party but everything happened so quickly."

After a week I received a letter from Mr. Taneja. He was having a great time with his new Indian wife. It was quite easy for an experienced and seasoned person like him.

The tone of his sermons to inexpert people like us was well maintained, "Don't put great ideas in women's minds. They get upset with great thoughts. Women look forward to meeting daredevils who don't make a fuss of every petty damn thing. Give them a feeling of security, assure them secrecy and provide them privacy and they will completely surrender before you…"

My friend took the letter forcibly from my hands. He remarked enviously, "This man has gone mad. He has become weird talking about women all the time. There are other meaningful jobs also to attend."

I started defending Mr. Taneja. A week later I was anxiously waiting for his next letter.

∞

Where Rainbows End

Mr. Shukla returned from Lahore two weeks back.

The memories of each and every moment spent there were still bright in his mind. He never felt tired or bored telling his neighbours and other known persons about his implausible stay in Lahore. He mentioned the real purpose of his visit to Lahore only to his few selected friends.

During the partition of the country, Mr. Shukla along with his large kinfolk had migrated from Lahore to Delhi.

He recalled proudly that they had such a large and elegant house at Lahore. His father was a professor at the Government College there. His uncle was a renowned advocate and his grandfather was a retired District Collector.

Mr. Shukla retired from the post of Chief Engineer from Railways some twenty-five years ago. He had only one daughter who was married to a Class One officer posted at Kolkata. His grandson was a software engineer in America. Wherever there was any of his relative he was highly placed, none was poor or a petty clerk.

Maybe someone might be there but Mr. Shukla never mentioned about him to anyone. He took pride in boasting about his rich and well-placed relatives.

Whenever a person would be sitting with him and suddenly the mobile of Mr. Shukla would ring, he would start boasting about the person to whom he was talking, "This was a call from my friend Mohan Singh. When I was posted as a Track Supply Officer on Simla-Dharampur railway line, Mohan Singh was a big contractor of that area dealing with government supply of wood to railways. One day I had just retuned to the station after an inspection by the trolley, an up-to-date Sardarji greeted me at the station giving me an attractive bouquet. I was surprised as there was no occasion for that. Anyway, I accepted it and said that we are not known to each other. Pressing my hand Sardarji remarked, 'If we are not known then now onwards we will be, since we are in the same line. You are newly posted here. I am in the government contract business. Both of us will have a great company.' I took him to my cabin."

Pausing for a while Mr. Shukla continued, "When I listened to the crooked designs of that man in my chamber, I couldn't control my anger. Still keeping my cool I said to him, 'Look Sardarji, you seem to be a sophisticated and refined person so I won't misbehave with you. Perhaps you don't know about me. Ask any damn person in Railways as to what reputation Mr. Manohar Lal Shukla holds. You have shown your character. This is our last meeting. I never adopted any corrupt practice in my whole life, then how at the fag end of my glorious career should I come in your crooked fold? Please go.' Mohan Singh said in a cool and collected manner, 'Mr. Shukla, perhaps you are unaware of my reputation here. I was trying to know your likes and dislikes. You judge yourself my dealings and then tell me how long our relationship would last.' Really Mohan Singh was a gem. He was really a very honest man like me and an accomplished contractor. His family was in this business since the British period. These days he lives in a 4-kanal house in our city. His son has an A-one imported furniture showroom in Karol Bagh. We are very good friends. He comes often and I too go to his Gurgaon farmhouse and enjoy his lavish parties."

It is very difficult to impress Mr. Shukla. He has his own classy stories to tell. He lives in his four bedroom flat in Gulmohar Group Housing Society. He has every luxury in his flat.

There are innumerable antique and impressive items in his collections. One of his maid servants spends two hours daily in dusting and cleaning those items. Mr. Shukla takes a deep interest in getting his flat cleaned and swept. When he goes out of station, he gets his furniture, sofa, chairs etc. covered with special polythene covers.

His second maid comes thrice in the day and prepares meals for him. Mr. Shukla's lunch and dinner timings are fixed. He takes two pegs of whiskey before dinner. He has got a small bar in his master bedroom.

He finishes his dinner by 9. He takes his breakfast strictly at 8 in the morning and must get his lunch at 1 in the afternoon. Wherever Mr. Shukla would go, he would keep his eyes on his watch and will get up five minutes before 1 p.m. He is very fond of morning walk. Rain or storm, he never misses it.

His best friends know well that Mr. Shukla was a passionately romantic person in his youth. Still now few people are familiar with his bohemian lifestyle. When his wife Suman was alive, she had a good check on his wayward activities.

He was living quite happily with his wife. And then his rough days came. Suman was diagnosed having breast cancer. Mr. Shukla took her frequently to Mumbai for treatment. He had no faith in the doctors of Delhi. One breast of Suman was removed. She started losing hair due to chemotherapy.

He ordered a special wig for her from a foreign country. Suman was very fashionable. She was from a family of politicians. She sported a rich jewellery of costly diamonds.

He was lucky to save his wife from cancer but she lost her life in a car accident. A truck hit her car and she died on the spot.

Mr. Shukla wept wildly and was not in his senses for one year. After that he became somewhat normal. He went to live with his daughter in Kolkata but came back after one month. He felt comfortable only in his own house.

After the death of his wife there came a sea change in the lifestyle of Mr. Shukla. Money was not a problem for him. He sold some shares of blue chip companies and bought a brand new luxury car. He took membership of golf club.

Only this year he went on a ten-day holiday trip to Singapore. It was heard that Mr. Shukla took his maid Maya along with him.

To avoid any scandalous rumour he remains a bit reserved with Maya. Maya is quite a young and smart woman.

The ladies of the society circulated this gossip that Mr. Shukla had given the precious clothes and costly jewellery of his wife to his maid Maya. She takes a good care of him and he too has a pleasant inclination for her.

Mr. Shukla is not a religious person in the strict term but in any religious or social gathering in the society, he is the first one to arrive. He doesn't sleep during daytime. He watches television or hunts over sexy and interesting sites on the internet. He passes his day by reading journals and newspapers. In the evening, he teaches needy children of poor families in a nearby municipal school free of cost.

He is very popular and trendy among young and sophisticated ladies of the society. He always remains at their beck and call.

Any lady can take help from him be it taking children to school in his car or seeing off their relatives to railway station or airport. In any function like kitty party, birthday, New Year, Holi or any other celebration, he participates very actively.

Last year there were many cultural activities after the Annual General Meeting of the society. Mr. Shukla won all the major prizes of senior citizen category. In Musical Chairs competition, he won from the young people too.

He remarked, "There is a secret formula to win in the musical chairs race. The leaders are very perfect in this game. The *funda* is to run slowly and cautiously. Keep your alert eye on the nearest chair and you won't lose."

In North India, there are a few months of extreme climates. The summers are unbearable and winters are chilly and difficult. In these months, he goes either to Mumbai or to Kolkata.

He says proudly, "There also I start getting bored after a month. Life is very fast there. Everyone is damn busy. They have no time for an oldie like me. They give me a car and a driver. I also feel like making merry, drinks or ladies, but before their driver I don't dare. But somehow I send away the driver on some pretext and manage some moments of pleasure and frolic. Mumbai is totally different from Delhi. Kolkata is really grand. You spend a few bucks more and a smart and cute young lady is at your service. You might be surprised that how a man of eighty can pine for and satisfy a lady of thirty. Gentlemen! Men and horses remain youthful and sturdy till death. You may or may not have sex but being with a young and beautiful lady is so loving and romantic that it, in itself, gives a fabulous stimulus. As a woman grows old, she loses interest in sex. On the other hand, a man's inquisitiveness and lust increases with age. Nature has developed this system to see that there should be no shortage of male for a growing female. Sex keeps us active and live. And if you mix feelings of love, romance or passions while enjoying sex with a lady then your interest in life is sustained and increased. Moreover if the lady is gorgeous then it is immaterial whether you have sex with her or not. In Singapore, I met and had a great time with a woman in her late forties. She was ready to come with me to India. She was from a nice Punjabi family. I told her that on my next visit I will take her to India. Singapore is very far. You can't go there often. At first thought I decided to keep her at Mumbai but at my age now I can't take these risky adventures too far."

Last year Mr. Shukla decided to visit Lahore. He said, "Nostalgia gripped me. In my dreams, I would always go to the streets, markets, college and other places of Lahore and its neighbouring towns. Then one day I wrote a letter to the present owner of our house at Lahore that I wanted to see the house of my forefathers and if the house has not been demolished and constructed afresh then my long cherished dream of sixty years would be fulfilled. These days the Delhi-Lahore bus service is fantastic and my nephew is a Class One officer in the Ministry of External Affairs."

After a sip from his glass, he continued, "I got a reply after a month. A phone number was given. I rang up. Sakeena Ahmed was speaking from Lahore. She was my batch mate in Sanatan Dharam College Lahore. I called her Sakku. We were deep in love with each other. It was she who taught me the first alphabet of love. There was an intensity in our love only due to the reason that we knew we won't be able to marry each other. After partition in 1947, I came to Delhi and that mad Sakku bought our house. She told me on the phone that she had kept all my things intact. She waited for years to get my contact number. One never forgets one's first love. It has a unique hold on our mind. When I met her after half a century, I found myself in teenage again. With her I walked tirelessly all the day in the streets of Lahore where I had spent my early days of life."

Heaving a deep sigh Mr. Shukla remarked, "You better know about the physical geography of a seventy-nine year-old woman. In a week's time I felt bored there. There was a gap of sixty long years between us. She had royal parents. After the death of her husband she got a rich property from him too. I told her that had I known about her ten years back I would have married her and brought her to India. Sakku said that she was still waiting for me. But due to the fear of my daughter and this society, I ran from Lahore. Here my life is one of complete freedom and fun. By bringing Sakku here I don't want to raise hurdles in my joyful and carefree life. Life can't be lived on sentiments only. Now when I receive the call of Sakku, I tell her that I will come to Lahore to bring her after the marriage of my grandson. And I know that I will not go there again."

Saying this Mr. Shukla raised his glass and started looking at the bubbles. With a twinkle in his eyes, he started humming a very old Hindi film song, "*Ye zindagi ke mele kabhi kam na honge, afsos hum na honge* (The festivities of life will go on. Alas! We would no longer be there)."

A River on Fire

She had resolved this time that she won't let it happen again. Rita was confident.

But it happened. Not once but thrice and it took place at the different periods of her life.

She was in her teens and quite innocent when she was raped. The first time it happened she was not even in her senses. The man had mixed some intoxicant in the coffee he offered to her.

Her grandpa had expired and her parents had to go to a far-flung city. Rita had to stay with her neighbour. Her entrance test for admission in a medical college was scheduled that week.

She was a protected child right from her childhood. Her mom never took any chance with her, never allowing her to go to the market or to a friend's house all alone. She studied in a girl's school and went to a women's college after matriculation.

Whenever their door bell rang, it was her mother who always opened the door. Rita was not sent to live with her relatives, she was stopped from going on school picnics and before dark she was shut in the inner boundary of her house. She was kept like a well-guarded secret or a treasure.

Her mom had left her alone for the first time. Rita was more fretful and worried about her exam. On that ill-fated night, she was preparing for her exam in her neighbour's house.

At around 12, Sham uncle came to her room and urged her to go to sleep. She told him that she had to revise certain topics and moreover the paper was in the afternoon, so she would go to sleep by herself. Uncle offered to make coffee for her.

It was that cup of coffee that changed her world. She got unconscious after taking the coffee. Around 10 in the morning, she woke up frighteningly and had a feeling of wetness around her legs.

She recollected that only a fortnight ago she was free from menses, then how could she get them again? She also discovered some bruises around her breasts and sex organ. In a moment, she was sure that uncle Sham had raped her by making her unconscious through the cup of coffee.

But who would believe her? What could she do? Should she raise a finger on the next door neighbour? Her mom was not there. If she complained to aunt regarding the misdeed of Sham uncle, she would not listen and agree with her. She would blame Rita instead.

Moreover, after a few minutes, she had to rush to take exam — the final test to become a doctor, a dream she had cherished right from her childhood. She kept mum. She had to pay a heavy price for that silence. She lost her balance and confidence and could not qualify the test. She had to be contented to become a staff nurse.

Next time when the catastrophe shook her, she was not silent. She rocked the whole nation. Even Parliament was shocked. Her issue was discussed there.

This time the rapist not only abused her sexually but had also tried to choke her voice too. She had managed to save herself somehow. And in that struggle she lost one eye.

The media raised the issue for a long time and the victimiser, a ward boy of her hospital was arrested and awarded capital punishment.

Rita was not satisfied with all that. She tried to commit suicide but then she decided to live to see her rapist hanged.

In an irrational offer the public, the press, the entire judiciary and enforcement machinery was stunned. The court had honoured the silly proposal of the rapist that he was ready to marry Rita, the woman he raped.

How could a rape victim marry her rapist and live happily with him? Many times before too, the court suggested reconciliation between the rapist and the injured party by allowing a marriage between them. But the parties should be of equal status.

In Rita's case, the man who proposed to marry was just a ward boy. Rita was a postgraduate in nursing. There was no match between them. He simply wanted to escape punishment.

Rita was burning with madness and anger. How could she give her consent to live for life with a person who ruined her self-esteem, who encroached upon her privacy and battered her body?

Was she a sheep or a cow? It was on hearing such a ridiculous proposal that Rita became so furious and tried to immolate herself. At last, the victim was hanged.

The worst part was that this time her rapist had smashed her self-respect while she was in her senses. Rita had not yet forgotten her teenage nightmare when a person known to her abused her so ghastly. Now she was raped in her senses just before her open eyes by a habitual rapist and that too when she was on her night duty. After her first rape she had vowed that she won't let it happen again but now that confidence was lost.

This time the rapist tied her feet and hands for he was a 'trained' rapist and had raped many other nurses and young patients. The other nurses kept mum for fear of ruining their reputation.

Rita was not that stuff. Now she had had enough of that humbug. A woman is not a dirty bitch that any stray and spoilt dog can sniff her ass.

She agreed to keep herself alive only to see the end of her rapist this time. In her teens, she wasn't aware enough to drag that bastard neighbour to law. But now this was the limit.

When the judiciary gave her a chance to reconcile with the guilty and asked for a marriage she was traumatised and devastated.

Where could she go now? The society took no lesson from her plunder. For centuries, the woman had been subjected to this cruel oppression and exploitation. She had lost all sentiments of justice, liberty or equality in her legal battle with male-dominated society.

She accepted no compensation from the court or the government. The government asks the nursing staff to work day and night attending howling patients but provides no security to them. They can easily fall prey to sex-starved patients, their relatives, ward boys or doctors.

She only requested to be transferred to a remote place. She decided to devote herself to the poor, needy and neglected people.

And then it happened for the third time. This should have been the end of life for her but she survived through this disaster.

The rapist this time was her hospital in-charge, the senior most doctor. He coaxed her, "Look dear, I know you have passed through a difficult time. Some things should better be forgotten. You have such a nice and sexy body, enjoy yourself. Don't burn yourself pointlessly. The man who wronged you was hanged. Don't waste your youth this way. Bury the past and enjoy the present."

Rita replied firmly, "Sir, I have burnt myself in this hell fire twice before. Don't try to push me to this furnace a third time or I will kill myself." The doctor didn't deter.

And for the third time, she was raped by her doctor. But after that Rita took a different turn. She made no complaint to the cruel world. She contacted her rapist the next night too and had a hearty sex with him.

The doctor was overjoyed. This went on for two months. And all of a sudden, the people all around were stunned to hear the news of suicide by Rita.

She had consumed poison at her residence. The police came and made enquiries. Rita's colleagues had suspicions on the senior most doctor, since he had developed intimate relations with her. The police found a suicide note. It read like this —

"I, Rita, am ending my life on my own, and for this, Doctor Manchanda should not be held responsible. It is true that he raped me two months ago. I had forewarned him not to plunge into me, for I was a stinking river on fire. But he didn't stop. He stirred my tranquillity. I punished him in my own way since I had no faith in social judicial system. I surrendered my body to him for a few days. Then from an AIDS patient, I injected the infection in my body and continued making sexual contact with the doctor. After a short time, I took his blood sample on some excuse and when it was confirmed that he was HIV positive, I thought my revenge was taken, and then I ended myself. Doctor Manchanda is suitably punished. He should be spared. He killed me and I finished him. Let it be an eye-opening incident for all those who think woman a lavatory to shit any time they get an opportunity."

The Beginning of an End

Saurabh never understood me. We were pitted against each other in the first year of our marriage.

He was never my man.

And then, I too became revengeful. I ceased to be his faithful wife.

I learnt those dirty tricks from him. I thought if he could hanker after countless women including his brother's wife, why should I lag behind?

I had more freedom, opportunities and time. I got full nine months of freedom from him when he was away on the ship.

It was not my dream to marry a rich boy. I was good at studies and was confident that I would be selected as an Air Hostess. I was tall, smart and gorgeous.

My parents were blinded by Saurabh's enormous wealth.

I, at that time, was youthful and ambitious, and was studying in Saint Xavier College. Proposals for my marriage were pouring in from all sides. My flawless beauty was quite an asset for me.

But now, I think painfully that my husband was such a worthless fellow that he never valued my beauty. He was awfully rich and swollen with pride. His lust was insatiable.

I don't know where I failed. Perhaps Saurabh, never took me in confidence, be it a matter of finance, children's education, relatives or family matters. He preferred to have his way in every matter and there grew my rancour and resentment against him.

On other fronts too, he was cruel and callous. He had developed a strange dislike and hatred for my parents, sister and brother.

He had this lurking fear in his mind all the time that I would give his money to my relatives. He picked up flimsy and petty quarrels to prevent their entry to his house.

In the beginning, I was a novice. I could not know his sinister designs. He created such a mess that I stopped going to my parents.

He wanted to make me like him — a selfish and crooked fellow. In the matter of finance, he was very exacting, cunning, hard task master and straightforward.

He made me write in a diary an account of every penny I spent. He would check and audit it, checking totals, snubbing and scolding me on every item of expenditure.

I would stand before him as a humble accountant and he would demand explanations like a stubborn and tyrannical boss.

The things, however, became a little tolerable when my son Nikhil was born. He was loved by all. The first male baby in the family is always a source of affection for everyone. But after three years, when my daughter Adhya was born, my position in the house started deteriorating.

Saurabh's attitude towards me became more and more arrogant, irritating and irksome. My status should have been like that of a mistress but he treated me like a maid.

He would intentionally do things that enraged me. By now, I had become more assertive and demanding about my rights and my rank.

Saurabh expected me to be a servant in the garden, a cook in the kitchen and a whore in the bed. I did all these roles perfectly well but his expectations rose very high, and still higher and higher.

I was never on the stable ground. After the death of my mother-in-law, my father-in-law had brought her mistress, his long time office colleague Mohini, to this house. She unleashed a despotic rule in the house, and so my position was threatened even further. She had a young daughter, Kalpana. They would live lavishly like queens while I was living with all the hardship.

I still remember the day when my father-in-law Mr Randhir Kashyap had come to our city for the finalisation of my marriage with Saurabh.

He and his relatives were wonderstruck seeing my height, complexion, style, beauty and my qualifications. They were looking for this type of girl — a bit fair, bold and pretty, but a little homely and submissive too.

Saurabh was then Second Engineer in the Merchant Navy. He drew a big salary. They had a big flat in this metropolitan city and they were distantly related to our family.

My doctor aunt lived in Delhi. She had cautioned me, "Look Ambika, we people are from small towns. Our approach and thoughts are still traditional and a bit conventional too. You are getting married in a modern family where there are no inhibitions in their minds and there is so much openness. You may face many challenges but if your husband is with you, you will clear all those obstacles. You will have to adjust and make a habit to stay without your husband for months together. Your husband travels in the whole world and you have not gone beyond Delhi. He must be cunning and more worldly wise."

Winking a mischievous eye, she said further, "People say that at every port, there awaits a wife for a merchant navy officer. They have handfuls of dollars in their pockets and a sinister lust in their brains. You will have to be very cautious. Marrying him would be like walking on a razor edge. Your only advantage is your awesome beauty and good nature. If you hold him tightly to your heart through your charming looks and good behaviour, then you will be happy. They say, in high seas, there live enchanting fairies that make the rich and young sailors forget their way to home. You will have to guard your husband against those menacing vamps."

How right was my aunt? If I could say 'no' to marriage at that stage, I would have saved my emotional balance. But I was charmed by the riches of my husband.

My father-in-law too had a charming personality. He pleaded my parents, "I have everything, sir. Give your pretty girl to us. We will keep her like a princess. Saurabh has left everything on me. He has only one condition and that is the girl should be majestic and elegant. We saw thousands of girls but Ambika is the sweetest of all and worthy to become my daughter-in-law.

We have common relatives and we liked your family. So please say 'yes' at once, my son is coming this month and we want to finalise his marriage this time."

With great imaginings, expectations and hopes, I had entered the dream house of my husband.

Only a day before the actual marriage, I met Saurabh at the *shagun* ceremony.

I was thinking that this man must be great, who had left the decision of his marriage on his father. I saw him. He was very cute, exhibiting royal charms.

In the ceremony, we were surrounded by numerous persons from both sides. I did not find a single moment when I could talk and judge Saurabh.

On the much awaited marriage night, Saurabh really impressed me.

He showed refined tastes and manners. He told me in details about each and every member of his family.

He told many things clearly, "Look Ambika, you have come from a small town. As time will pass, you will come across many odd things in this house. This is because we live in a big city. You will have to keep your mouth, eyes and ears closed for the time I am at sea. I can't come overnight in case of any emergency. If someone comes and relieves me and when the ship reaches near a shore, only then I can fly back to home to attend to your complaint. Moreover, every time I have to execute a contract with my company for almost eight or nine months a year. If I come back in the middle of the contract, the loss is ours."

He praised me a lot and vowed to keep me like a queen throughout his life.

He added, "You will not bother yourself with what others say or what others do. I will fix your pocket money and you will get that amount on 1st day of every month."

He kept his promise literally. I never had any difficulty, especially financial one, and that was the reason I stayed in the house till now.

It was much later that I realised what a cunning fellow he was in reality. A seasoned and clever person as he was, he couldn't ditch his wife for long.

He knew the weakness of people around him, be it his brother or his father. Everyone supported him since he was a hen who laid golden eggs daily. His income was in millions.

I was under this impression that Saurabh would always remain a slave to my beauty and charms. That was my failing and misapprehension.

He would get annual leave of four months. Till his first leave after marriage, he paid his full and best attention to me. In the days that followed, I came to know many distressing tales about him. But I just ignored those trivial matters. I thought that before marriage, every man has a different life. Now that I have come, I will put the things right.

Saurabh had little faith in me. He kept all secrets to his heart. How much he earns, how much he spends or invests, he never gave me any clue or details.

During his stay on the ship, he phoned me occasionally. With his brother or father, he would talk for hours, giving them instructions and getting information from them daily.

His younger brother Gaurav was not good at studies. So Saurabh and his father had purchased some agricultural land in a nearby village where they were planning to set up a factory or a farmhouse in order to settle Gaurav.

After Saurabh came back after the first year of our marriage, I realised that he was not the same Saurabh I was married to.

He was a person full of haughtiness, vanity and conceit. He showed his true colours now.

I did not know that he was a sexually perverted person. He didn't relish normal sex.

My aunt was right. A sailor gets chance to expose himself to a variety of sexual fantasies, orgies and fancies.

I was a simple girl. I knew nothing about the ultra-modern ways of living and enjoying life.

It was monsoon season when he came back from sailing. He brought so many beautiful presents for all of us. For me, he himself was a unique present.

In the evening, both of us took our dinner at the *Piccadilly*. He gulped down a few pegs of whisky and forced me to drink too. I hardly gulped down one such peg just to please him.

I had never taken alcohol. There was no such tradition in my parental home. There, men were teetotallers.

He forced me and mixed it with a cold drink. My head started whirling. He gave me another peg too. To please him, I gulped it down.

Then I don't know where he took me. It was perhaps his friend's house. I was unconscious. I don't exactly remember what happened there.

I later discovered that he had a circle of high society friends who organised wife-swapping parties. Since I took no interest in those nonsensical couples, he never took me there again.

At around midnight, I came to my senses. I was in my own bedroom. Saurabh was sipping wine from his glass. I was wonderstruck to think that he had consumed a large quantity of wine at the hotel and now at this time of the night too, he was drinking again. He was so mad for wine.

I tried to advise him and he agreed. He put off the light. He came to my bed.

A strong smell was coming from his mouth but I didn't think it better to stop him. He had come back home after eight months.

He was drunk and tired, but full of desire.

His eyes were red. His sex was strange and wild. Despite my inhibitions, he forced me to suck him. I felt like vomiting. But in my heart of heart, I was hopeful that at least now I would have power over him. He did unnatural sex with me. I cried with pain but he took more joy in that.

I was mistaken. He was very calculating and undomesticated too. I failed to tame him.

*

Saurabh, my husband slipped out of my hands. I tried every talisman, trick, skill and tactic. I perfected myself in cooking. I wore latest clothes, I improved my accent. I made my children work hard and shine in their studies.

He would come back after eight or nine months from sailing and would rock the house.

He would snub every person with one plea only, "You know how I face challenges in the roaring sea all the time. I remain shut in my small cabin and work hard day and night to earn this money on which you people enjoy like anything. I pay a heavy price for it."

He would frown and fret. He would clench his fists and roar, "Every year I plan not to go back to that bloody killing sea. I decide to start a business over here but when I calculate that you people spend so lavishly here and that my income in Indian rupees would not be sufficient to support you, I go back again to that hell. At this age, I can't remain awake all night and give so tough duty."

I would argue, "There are many other navy officers like you in the city. I talk to their wives. They do not complain like this."

"They have good and sympathetic people at their homes. They don't have nagging and fastidious wives like you."

"They confide in their spouse, give them all they earn and they are sincere in their character. I know the character of these modern women going to clubs and kitty parties. They dote on each other's husband. You know what your problem is. You think yourself too smart, rather over smart. I have ample proofs of your infidelity. I have seen with my own eyes the messages in your mobile phone. You are a menace before my eyes, what must be your profile when you go to Mumbai and abroad."

How long could I argue with such a clever fellow?

Nikhil and Adhya were not kids. They knew the tales of flirting of their dad. They had all information about his bohemian style of living. They were convinced that their dad was a big cheat. To cover up his bad deeds, he would keep all of us in a state of perpetual tension.

There was his baser instinct behind this. It was his true nature. His dad was also like this.

Sometimes he would melt down. But for that I would have to pay a heavy price. He would seduce and wring me like a dog. He would ask for strange conditions for the petty favours.

Though he earned a lot but he was miser of first water. He won't buy good clothes for himself and when a social function or a marriage of close relative or neighbour would come, he would wear those old-fashioned and worn-out attire that he had worn for many years.

When I would complain, he would say in front of all, "Your husband may be rich, but I am a poor man. I won't get any pension after I retire. I have to be a miser. I see many Ship Captains who go to sea even at the age of sixty-five. Their wives and children don't leave anything for their old age."

We were not included in his schemes of things. I had to carve out a life for me myself.

When I saw that his wealth being plundered by Mohini and her lustful daughter Kalpana, I started asking an account of Saurabh's income.

I said to him, "Okay Saurabh, don't give me any previous account prior to my marriage with you but now onwards I must know what your income, expenditure and savings are."

I stated plainly, "Now, you are married. Your children need good education. If you will continue giving your earnings to everyone else, how will you manage your household?"

For a few months, he went on delaying discussion on this topic.

One night when he was dead drunk, he told me about his financial management, "Look Ambika, I am the elder son of this house. Dad has retired. He is happy with his new wife. I have to think about my younger brother. We have purchased agricultural land. There we plan to start dairy and herbal farming. In coming years, we shall have a good return on this investment. I have to invest more in this venture."

I interrupted, "For the past ten years, you have earned more than fifty million rupees. And that has all gone nowhere. The land that you have purchased is not even in your name. Tomorrow, if something happens to you, then I will have to beg from your younger brother."

He became furious, "I am insured for millions, and you won't have to worry if I die. As regards our family business, you don't know ABC of anything. So you better shut your mouth. I fix your monthly expense as twenty thousand rupees. That is all."

"How will I manage my kitchen, children's fees, and car and the driver, electricity bills and…"

"Okay, I make it thirty."

"No way, give me your cheque book. I will make all payments through that."

"It is not possible. Okay, I will give you fixed pocket money of fifty thousands."

"How much you get in a month?"

"Now, that is none of your concern."

"A wife must know how much her husband earns."

"I earn two and a half lakh rupees per month."

"So you'll give me just fifty thousand and keep two lakhs with you every month."

"I told you our farmhouse..."

"It is not ours, it is theirs."

"You are a fool to think me a naïve person."

"You are not naïve. You are cunning and over smart. You keep this money to make merry in your vacations."

"How can you say?"

"I know your adventures and misadventures, especially your darling ladies on whom you spend like an Arab Sheikh spends on his harem."

"You have gone crazy. You are levelling charges on your sincere husband."

"I have seen with my own eyes."

"What have you seen?"

"You were embracing Kalpana in the car. You get phone calls from so many ladies. If I remain mum that doesn't mean I can't make out what you do when you return after midnight from late night parties and golf clubs."

"You are a crab. You are crooked having the mentality of lower middle class people. You are an old-fashioned woman from a small town, jealous of my modern lifestyle. For ten months, I work on the ship day and night and toil round the clock just like a donkey. For a month or so, I come here to relax and you bloody orthodox bitch make my life a hell. I will do whatever I like."

"I won't let you have your autocratic way."

"You will stop me. You, a pauper, a parasite, a small fry! You will stand against Saurabh Kashyap, the Chief Engineer in Merchant Navy, getting a tax free salary of three lakhs a month."

He gave me a severe blow.

On that day, he raised his hand on me for the first time. And for the last time too. I didn't give him another opportunity.

He slapped me, kicked me and threw me on the ground. He was mad with anger. He was drunk and had all his wits out. He tried to strangle me.

I too resisted against him and pushed him to the wall. He could hardly stand on his own since he was drunk. I started yelling at a high pitch. But, who would have come at my rescue?

Those present in the house were his paid and loyal men. They were prospering on his money. Why would they stop him?

I wept and cried, and he became more annoyed. Once again, he slapped me. I yelled wildly.

He increased the volume of the television and beat me like a cow. I was wonderstruck at his brute behaviour.

After he thrashed me, I didn't utter a word to anyone. To whom could I complain?

I came back to my bedroom and kept thinking and brooding how I could save my family from the ruin. I had to take care of my children too.

And that was not possible without financial help from Saurabh.

During his entire leave period, I didn't go to his bedroom. We were not on talking terms. When we would come in front of people, we addressed and talked to each other.

When he went back to the ship, he didn't call me. He kept on sending me the pocket money so that domestic work didn't suffer. We remained strangers to each other.

That was the most depressing period of my life. I had a husband whom I could not call my own. He didn't even talk to Nikhil or Adhya. He had become so stonehearted. We were sitting in hostile camps and living like enemies. We were bent upon forcing the other party to surrender.

And that was the starting point of my rebellion against him.

*

No one in the house talked to me now. They got a reason to hate me. They thought me their enemy, since I was on the drive to check my husband from paying them huge money.

I had a car and a driver. The children were in good schools. The maids helped me to make the children ready for the school. When the children came back from their schools, the tuition madam was ready to teach them. I had no tension of any kind, except the altercations with my husband.

I had time and time. I had thoughts and thoughts. There was no end to my sufferings. I had lost interest in everything. I didn't go either to beauty parlour or to shopping. I had lost interest in sex too. With whom I could enjoy it.

I would sit in the dark corner of my bedroom and would brood over the pandemonium between Saurabh and me. How long will this tussle between us continue? Does it affect him? Is he not worried about his children at all? I was strongly of this view that at least for our children's sake, he would make a truce with me. Has he no feelings for them? The children asked me daily why papa didn't call us. I replied them that he was at a place where he couldn't contact us.

I thought, really has that stage set in where he won't come back to me? In the hope of a positive response from him, I passed those eight months. If not for me, he would surely reconcile for the sake of our children. People say that children are like bridges between a husband and his wife.

It was the time for his annual leave. He could come anytime.

I thought of many options. Should I forgive him easily? How long could I continue that bitter battle against him?

He didn't come.

I thought he had extended his contract with the company to serve a few months more. He was doing it intentionally just to torment and tease me so that I might break down, apologise, and implore him to come.

I thought, "If I surrender, he would be a despot again, beating and bullying me every third day. No, I won't let him thrash me again. I am an honourable lady. If he leaves me, I can still get a good gentleman. He beat me for no fault of me. Moreover, he subdued my status in the house. He went back without informing me. He didn't enquire about me or about our children for the past one year, and even then I beg pardon from him. I am not a fool. Pardon! My foot! He can't refuse my maintenance money. Let me see how long he will ignore me."

One day, my old time college fellow Manju met me in the market. Her husband was a high-ranking officer and was posted in the city recently.

Manju called me another day. She invited me to a kitty party at a hotel.

All her nice friends and other pretty ladies had come. I was feeling a bit better going there. I saw a new world there — the way women expressed themselves and passed their time in a friendly and affable get-together was wonderful.

My social circle expanded. Now I regularly started going to these social gatherings and kitty parties. We ate at best restaurants, played *tambola* and developed new links.

When I started moving out, my interest in life revived. I kept myself up-to-date, visited beauty parlours and fashionable boutiques, wore latest clothes, and got smarter and smarter.

I started going to Manju's house often. She would come to my residence too. She had a lovely daughter. Manju's husband Ashok was a jolly good fellow.

We were a group of friends now partying every week on one pretext or the other. We would play *tambola*, sing songs, went on picnics to nearby hill stations, and visit trendy malls and multiplexes.

No news of Saurabh came and one and a half year elapsed. But I was emotionally stable. I had many good friends and Manju was my best friend. I would stay there till late evening. She would call her friends and we would have a great time. Their husbands also participated in these get-togethers.

And then I got that shocking and awful news. I met the wife of a friend of Saurabh who was also in the Merchant Navy. She told something strange and appalling. Her husband had told her that Saurabh was staying in Mumbai for the last two months. A lady was also seen staying with him in a hotel.

That was my first shock, a jolt I could never forget all my life.

I decided to take a revenge on him.

Now I scratched his name from my heart.

I was living in a locality where there were not many inhibitions.

If Saurabh could live his life normally falling apart from me, I was a damn fool to sacrifice my youth and vigour for an immoral womaniser like him. I could also find a good partner and live happily.

It was then my outlook and attitude towards life changed. I wanted to avenge.

And it didn't take me much time and effort. I started my hunt.

It was not to satisfy my lust. It was to become my husband's equal. To surpass him in the race of infidelity and unfaithfulness, so that he may repent on his misdeeds.

I had a great liking for Manju's husband from the day I met him. He was a robust and dark-complexioned man, smart and stylish. He mixed up with me a lot, and many a time I had asked him to drop me at places where we friends had get-togethers and kitty parties.

Now I started taking more interest in him. I would intentionally phone him knowing well that Manju was not at home at that time. I started fancying having sexual relations with him.

And I got a chance to realise those fanciful dreams.

It was Christmas evening.

I was at Manju's residence. We were having a small get-together.

We had a few Christian friends there and they insisted for the dinner. We were cracking jokes, playing *tambola* and having fun. The time was passing in a pleasant way.

Before the dinner was served, we friends took a few pegs of red wine. Intentionally I took a bit extra. I had evil designs in my mind.

I had no experience with wine. I purposefully landed myself in a difficult situation. In that condition, I could not drive my way to home. I asked Manju to let her husband Ashok drop me in his car. She readily asked him.

It was pitch dark outside. That was a very chilly winter night.

My house was on the outskirts of the city. It was an hour's drive. There was a devil in my heart.

Ashok started the car and I sat very close to him. He too had taken a few pegs of wine.

I had become very bold after taking wine. He was driving fast.

I caught hold of his hand and said in a satirical tone, "You are going fast; I am not a burden that you want to get yourself rid of so soon."

He showed still more bold heart. He pressed my hand slowly, slowed down the vehicle, and remarked, "No ma'am, if you say, I will drive as slow as possible. What a beautiful and romantic night! The people are enjoying in the hotels."

He stopped the car in the dark corner of the road.

He kissed me lovingly. After a long period, I had the feel of a man. Ashok was a very romantic sort of person. He went on kissing me for a long time.

I was getting more and more impatient. The wine that we had gulped down was working wonders. I became braver and went nearer to him.

I embraced him more tightly and passionately. I slid my hand through his broad and hairy chest and started caressing it. His complexion was slightly dark and that turned me on and made me wild and crazy.

He was kissing my neck and murmuring praises about my beauty. I loved his sweet nothings. With my soft touches and caressing, he became hornier. I had not had such a great time for the last two years.

That night was really a great one, which opened the gates to my real womanhood.

Till now, I had believed that a woman belonged only to his husband alone, but now I realised my folly. A worthless husband who didn't know the value of his wife's love and didn't care for her tears must be dumped as soon as possible.

After that, I never remained depressed. My relations with my husband became a bit normal.

I had equalled him in the rivalry. He had made me like him — a stray animal. No morals, no guilt. I no longer cared for him. At last, he realised my worth but it was too late. The damage was already done. There was no looking back since then.

Saurabh came to know about this new me.

He was not shocked. He felt a bit relieved. No one was there to scold and nag him now. He had a free hand.

I had become tactful. There was no dearth of my admirers. I fancied around. Almost all my friends' husbands were at my beck and call. I didn't need to spend money on my lovers. I had a good advantage over Saurabh.

He had money. He could buy sex. He enjoyed young ladies.

When he would come on leave, he would request me to spend at least one night with him. He still loved my gorgeous body.

Now too, we fought as usual but we did not become annoyed with each other. He bargained with me. He would give me precious gifts in exchange of sex.

I don't know why he still wanted sex with me. Maybe, my wayward fancying around with other men had excited him. He would always plead me to try 'something different'. Really he was a great pervert.

My only remorse — he made me like himself. I still get a lot of money from him, but don't love him.

∞

Never Say Tomorrow

Mohan Lal's heart thumped heavily as he read that electrifying news on the first page of today's newspaper.

His friend had already told him about it but he had not anticipated that it would be announced so early.

He sat in his chair on the terrace of his third floor flat. It was his routine to get up early, prepare bed tea and wake up his wife. Together they sat in the balcony, read news, exchanged views and enjoyed their tea.

He placed the cups of tea on the table and called his wife.

It was a fine morning of early March. In North India, it is the most coveted weather. It is the time when mornings and evenings become very pleasant. The summers and winters are too severe and unbearable in this part of the country.

His wife came out yawning, rubbing her eyes and holding her spectacles in one hand.

Lifting the cup of tea, she remarked, "Let me also see today's newspaper. What is the lead news that has made you so sombre? Is the government falling?"

Mohan Lal became a bit uneasy and nervous as if he was caught concealing something from his wife. He controlled himself.

With a firm voice, he hissed, "Nothing remarkable. The same old gossips and news of road accidents and riots — three died, thirteen injured. What else is in newspapers these days, except the sensational exposures of leaders, scams or the doctor who sold hundreds of kidneys?"

For once Mohan Lal thought in his mind, "Let me tell my wife about that news. That will ease my burden." But then, he controlled himself. He found it better to be silent unless she discovered it herself.

He was of this firm belief that a man should conceal a serious thing from his wife. A woman could not digest bitter truths of complex life. Many a secret were buried deep in his heart. He thought his wife did not have courage to absorb those crude shocks.

His wife knew only that much about this world as much he disclosed to her. Whenever she heard something different or unusual thing not told by Mohan Lal to her, there would be fiery arguments between them. Such hot debates between the couple would always conclude with Mohan Lal's eternal sentence, "Leave it yaar, I am not an ass. I have seen the world."

Mohan Lal's small world was within the radius of eight miles — from his residence to his office and from his office back to his residence. All the known persons knew the small world known to him.

Mohan Lal handed his wife all the pages of the newspaper and involved her vehemently in a heated discussion about home and the world. He did not want her to catch that horrible news item. The thing, which should be suppressed, should remain so; otherwise it becomes a storm unnecessarily.

Then he ordered her to get up and start preparing his breakfast and the lunch tiffin. He made a flimsy excuse that an inspection team was scheduled to come to his office this afternoon from the Headquarters and that he was assigned the important duty of receiving them from the Railway Station and make other arrangements.

He carried the first page of the newspaper to the office.

Throughout the day, he was worried lest his wife may discover about that news item.

His wife had a hoard of informers in the neighbourhood. She always kept in touch with the latest information, rumour, gossip or hearsay in the colony. Every Tom, Dick and Harry had a cable television and mobile. It had become extremely difficult to a keep a secret well guarded these days.

To keep a track of the developments at home, Mohan Lal rang up his wife from his office phone.

His wife was very thrilled. She said in an excited voice, "Have you read today's main news?"

Mohan Lal's heart sank. His secret was out, he was sure. His face turned pale, voice more depressed and hands started trembling.

Still having a hope, thinking that maybe she was speaking of anything else, he reassured her, "Yes, yes! I had read all the news. There was nothing significant. The same old market rates, price of gold touching new heights and the sports and shares…."

His wife interrupted, "No, no! I am not talking about all that humbug. I was talking about our government hospital. I had gone to Mrs. Tiwari's house and she told me about the latest information of the news that the Chief Minister has inaugurated the special cardiac wing in the Hospital here. Now, the bypass surgery of heart could be done here itself. Doctors from Delhi will come twice a week and do these operations, and that too at much reasonable rates. It is a good news. Now there would be no tension."

Mohan Lal thought in his heart, "You don't know, it is going to be a big problem for me."

He tried to snub her, "Well, Delhi is after all Delhi, there are the best hospitals there, like Escorts and Apollo. The facilities there are of international level. Ours is a damn poor government hospital for the common man. They will cut and dissect the man and handover to you, and eventually you will have to rush to Delhi. I will still say that it will be foolish to have a heart surgery from here. Yaar, I have seen the whole world. Okay, we will discuss about it in the evening."

After he came back from his office, his wife, handing him a cup of tea, chirped, "I have telephoned *Babuji* to send uncle quickly. We will make his card from the Government Hospital and get the tests completed. *Babuji* was telling that uncle has made an arrangement of fifty thousands rupees and the rest… I told him proudly that he should not worry about money. My husband will take care of everything. He said that he would return the money very soon."

Mohan Lal placed the cup of tea on the table. In an irritated tone he shouted, "Is there my dad's bank here, from where I will take out one lakh rupees and get the surgery of your uncle done? I make it clear to you again that I won't touch my provident fund. Our own children have forgotten us. They are involved in their own families. No one knows when one catches a serious disease. Thousands are spent in a day. Tomorrow if I die suddenly, your own people will respect you only if you have good bank balance. In old age, wealthy persons get better respect."

Mohan Lal's wife maintained her soft voice, "Who else is there to take care of uncle? He didn't marry. He remained with *Babuji* all his life. Whatever uncle earned he spent there. There is good land in his name. That too will go to our family. Moreover, he is saying that he'll pay back within six months. He has great regards for you…."

Mohan Lal roared, "If he has such good regards for me then why doesn't he sell an acre of his land and bring one lakh rupees with himself to get the surgery done? Why is he bent upon exhausting my hard-earned money? My retirement is near. There is no hope from the children that they will lend me any money in emergency. They themselves have scarce resources."

His wife pleaded but Mohan Lal got more infuriated, "I have devoted my whole life in getting almost all of your relatives treated in good hospitals here. Now I am fed up. Please excuse me. Your uncle has other nephews. Why don't they come forward and pool the money? If there emerges an emergent need, only then I would withdraw money from my provident fund. Leave yaar, I am not an ass. I have seen the whole world."

Mohan Lal's wife maintained her cool. She knew the true nature of her husband. His temper would run very high all of a sudden and then after some time he would cool down and agree to her opinion. Wives have that tact. They know the pulse of their husbands. They force their husbands to accede to their odd whims and conceits.

Mohan Lal was thinking about something else. He was going to retire after three years. All his life, he could not save a single penny. He gave good education to his kids, purchased a flat and married off his kids. Now for the last few years, he had been saving some money in his provident fund account.

His wife's family lived in a nearby town. Those people always kept him in a tight corner. He tended with care every sick person who came to him from his father-in-law's house. He had a one bedroom flat. On many occasions, he had to place a folding bed in kitchen for himself so that the sick person could feel comfortable in his house. He had to carry the food for the sick to the Government Hospital daily. Sometimes one has to do all such odd things, but now it was the limit. How could he spend more than a lakh on the heart surgery of his wife's uncle?"

This matter was a subject of heated discussion between Mohan Lal and his wife. Once or twice, Mohan Lal thought of agreeing to his wife's proposal, but the very next day, he would change his mind.

In his office, people would narrate tragic tales of the unfortunate people who were foolish enough to fritter away their pension accumulations and provident fund money on their children and close relatives, and then they repented the rest of their lives. When in their old age, they fell seriously ill or needed surgery, they had to queue up before Red Cross Society or some other charitable institution to get the costly treatment. They didn't keep enough money for themselves even to buy a second hand car.

Mohan Lal and his wife didn't speak to each other the whole night. No dinner was prepared. Television was not switched on.

Both the sons of Mohan Lal were well settled in other cities. They also sometimes sought financial help from him. Mohan Lal's wife always fought with her both daughters-in-law on one pretext or the other. She had an inclination towards her parents' house. Those people always sought help from her through sycophancy and false praise. She had five real uncles, three sisters and two brothers in nearby towns, who would often come and stay at Mohan Lal's residence to disturb his peace of mind every now and then.

Only last year, a storm of this nature came in their lives when Mohan Lal's wife brought her nephew from her brother's house. She insisted that he should be admitted in a school here since he lagged behind in his studies in the town because of his bad company. Mohan Lal took a stern stand. He didn't take his meals for two days. Only then his wife relented.

Now once again that sort of a tense deadlock came between the couple.

In the morning, Mohan Lal got up as usual. He prepared bed tea and kept the tray in the balcony.

He called his wife, "Sudha, get up, newspaper has come. Get up and take tea."

His wife came out, rubbing her eyes, holding her spectacles. Mohan Lal was busy reading news. He was diffident to face his wife. A taut silence was stretched between them.

Sudha took a sip from her cup and said in a stiff and resolute voice, "I take your decision to be final. You are not going to take the money from your provident fund. Let us do one thing then. I will bring all my gold ornaments from the bank locker. That is my own treasure. No one has a claim on them. The rate of gold has soared to new heights. Let me sell them today and you proceed with the angiography of uncle tomorrow."

Hearing this, Mohan Lal's heart sank. His feet became cold. It seemed to him that the moment of his surrender had arrived. He would have to say yes to his wife now and fill the withdrawal form today for an advance from his provident fund. After all, he was not an ass. He had seen the world.

A Suitable Bride

My cousin Rajat is a weird fellow. It looks quite strange that he is over fifty and is still unmarried.

It is not that in his youthful days, he didn't get good proposals. He had a varied choice of girls but no proposal could materialise.

There are three reasons for a person like Rajat remaining unmarried despite having all other good traits and being a good husband material.

One reason may be that such persons did not have the time to plan a marriage. We do come across such people in our life who say that they don't have time enough even to die since they are damn busy. Only such persons live long and when they get time and leisure, they die with ease.

There was our old aunt, who too died with much ease and relaxed mood. So many times, she became seriously ill and the people around thought her dead. They placed her on the floor. All the near and dear ones were informed. But in the next few moments, the aunt got up alive, disappointing all of them. The relatives went back to their towns in sad and remorseful mood thinking that they will have to come again for all that. When the aunt died in the end, no one was near her. She was put in the pyre unceremoniously.

My dear brother Rajat had a lot of leisure and free time. He was working in an office, which had five days a week schedule. In the past so many years, he made use of these two holidays every week to hunt eligible girls for his marriage.

The second reason for not getting married at the right time may be heartbreak in a true love affair. Nowadays, heartbreak has become a thing of the past. The Romeo-Juliet type couple is a rare genus in this post-internet period. There is a least possibility of Rajat being involved in a love affair. He is not that stuff who wastes time on such worthless things.

The third reason why a person avoids marriage may be that he might be medically unfit i.e. an impotent. I don't doubt Rajat on that ground since he narrates many anecdotes where he made physical contacts with the girls he came across while hunting for the most suitable bride for him. Moreover, I am not the final authority in this matter.

I asked Rajat a number of times, "Dude, it is enough now. You have seen all the damsels and pretty women of this region. Now, take a final decision and get married. You have crossed fifty. Now stop that endless search. This long hunt has turned your hair grey."

He chirped, "Don't worry dear; I am getting a good choice. I saw a widow this week only. Through matrimonial columns, we were introduced. She is the only legal heir of a grand house valuing one crore rupees. We dated freely and merrily, and had a great fun. What else we wanted? But then all of sudden, one day, she said that she had found a billionaire widower. Moreover, our horoscopes didn't tally. No regrets! Only yesterday, I saw the only girl of a top class businessman. The girl is very sexy, smart and quite younger than me, but she has a slight defect in one eye. They are offering a super dowry, a twenty per cent share in their factory."

I said impatiently with concern, "Then my dear chap, why are you delaying the decision? Before anyone else should outsmart you, decide at once and go over with it. You have spent your whole youth in this mad game of witch hunting."

Rajat said cheerfully, "You will remain silly. Today I am going to meet a girl who is working as an Income Tax Officer. Being a *Manglik*, she could not get a suitable match in her twenties. Moreover, that crazy girl was in love with some IAS boy who ditched her. She is damn gorgeous. She has a big house, luxury car and a huge bank balance. If God willed, this time, I am sure I will get engaged."

I gave him an elderly advice, "Do whatever you want to do, but do it quick. Your hair has turned grey. After every week, you dye them. The children of your class fellows returned from their honeymoons since long, and there you are, the same old chap — still single and worn down. Marry at the earliest, otherwise you will repent later on when no one will come forward with any proposal. You have grown old and haggard. People lie when they say that a man and a horse seldom get old."

Such harsh words rarely have any effect on the big brother Rajat. Every Saturday and Sunday, he gets ready and moves out to look for a new would-be bride.

He has seen more than a hundred girls. Some of them were introduced to him in majestic hotels, in beautiful and lovely parks, on the lake, coffee houses, offices, and in would-be brides' houses.

He had become addicted to this fad of seeing girls one after another, rejecting the previous one and going passionately ahead with the next one.

Those days, this Hindi film's song was a big hit, "*Ek ladki ko dekha to aisa laga, jaise khilta gulab, jaise shayar ka khwab, jaise ujli kiran*... (When I saw a wonderful girl, I felt as if she were a budding rose, a poet's dream, a radiant ray of light....)"

With the unique qualities of the dream girl mentioned in the song, Rajat had a large variety of fairy girls all around. Through matrimonial columns of all the leading newspapers, bio-data and loveliest photograph of numerous eligible girls were scrutinised by Rajat. He would reject all of them in the hope that the next ones would be more promising. Some other good proposals of marriage were being suggested by some good families in their social circle. More than a dozen brokers of marriage bureaus were taking keen interest in him.

But now everyone was fed up of the ruckus created by Rajat. They requested him with folded hands, "Please sir, go this way or that way, get married soon. The prices of everything are soaring. Get tied in a matrimonial knot."

Rajat's father was a heart patient. It was his long cherished desire to see his clan increase. He had a strong desire to play with his grandchildren. Rajat was the only male child of his family.

His snobbery and confusion had reached the climax. He was thinking that the girl he would see the next day would surely be smarter than the previous one. There was certainly something special about all the girls he met. He hoped that the next one would be more gifted, more beautiful and from a richer family.

Whenever a new proposal came, Rajat's close relatives found fault with girl's background or her family, and then everyone said with one voice, "Mr. Rajat, you go and first see the girl, maybe you like her, we will decide about the family later on."

"*Ek ladki ko dekha*...," there was something magical about this song which inspired Rajat so much that after seeing every girl he would become even more excited and would expect a still more beautiful girl which he thought would be in his luck.

He found a few girls too good and gorgeous as per traits mentioned in this song. They were tall, blonde-haired, sexy, and full-bodied with large, heavy and firm breasts — an hourglass figure.

Rajat would say 'yes'. But his mom would mar the whole matter by saying, "The father of the girl is a petty superintendent in a small worthless government office. He is no match to our status. He won't arrange a fine marriage party. He will put us all in an embarrassing situation."

Where they would find a wealthy family, the horoscopes won't match.

Well, Rajat was in no hurry indeed. He had the same routine.

He would go and see at least two girls in a week. His complaints and naggings were right and justified to some extent.

He would grudge to me, "The girl's parents are big frauds these days. They boast about girls' qualities by exaggerating the facts. When I go, I find a totally different picture. They propose me to see the girl first. They don't tell me what cash they would give me in marriage, how much they will spend on the marriage party. They boast that the girl's uncle is an excise officer, he must be, what to me. I simply don't go to see the girl alone. All girls are of same stuff. They look alike. What other qualities, like financial status, they possess is more important to me."

On many occasions, I too accompanied Rajat in his usual visits to his prospective fathers-in-law's houses. We were welcomed. Delicious refreshments were served to us. We people would disperse in other rooms leaving only Rajat and his would-to-be bride alone to finalise the matter.

The scene would become more romantic when Rajat was left alone with the girl on the lake. They both would gracefully boat in the lake. The whole scene would look like the Hindi song of *Pakeeza*, "*Chalo dildar chalo, chand ke par chalo… Na kabhi khatam ho ulfhat ka safar* (O my love, let us go to the other side of moon…. This journey of love should never end.)"

Rajat wanted this process of continuously enjoying in the company of a new girl every third day to go for ever. What is there in a marriage? Millions of people marry and suffer all through their lives. To be in the company of a new girl every week, how romantic is this and how pleasant and enjoyable!

The elegantly dressed, magnificently looking, modest and humble girls would behave like a touch-me-not plant before him, looking like *Umrao Jaan* or *Anarkali*. And next week again, Mr. Rajat would be found in the company of a new fairy in a five star hotel. There would be a sparkling dazzle all around. After all, the question is of marriage of a well-placed rich Engineer.

Our uncle, Rajat's father, was looking for a cultured and homely girl from a respectable family but Rajat's choice was more important. That's why this process of hunting a suitable bride was going for the past 25 years. In two or three meetings with a girl, what could Rajat decide?

He had reached at the climax of confusion. He had become so upset and perplexed, expecting that the next girl he would see would certainly be the paragon of all virtues. But he would find one or two weak points in every family. In fact, he had grown old but he had not relaxed any of his conditions and other parameters for choosing the bride.

Well, every romantic tale has its tragic end. Rajat's romantic era too came to an end. His brother-in-law was watching these bohemian and flirtiest activities of Rajat since long. He was not relishing the way Rajat was leading a quixotic and royal life. He thought that this way Rajat would remain single throughout his life and that he never wanted.

His brother-in-law too was a great hunter in his youth. In the matter of searching girls for marriage, he too had rejected dozens of girls.

But Rajat played an active role in getting the marriage of his sister Suhasini fixed quickly with this brother-in-law. And that was the reason the brother-in-law now wanted a revenge of all that.

Eventually he was successful in his mission. He entangled Rajat in his relations. By chance, Rajat got an opportunity to stay in that city where his brother-in-law's cousin lived. She had a daughter whose marriage was also being delayed for one reason or the other. See the ill luck of Rajat; he stayed there for a month during his official training.

That proved a waterloo for Rajat. This time, he saw the girl quite closely and passionately. The lion was imprisoned and put in a cage.

Then that practice of bride hunting came to an end. Rajat was ceremoniously married and handed over to his wife. He and his wife were both in their early fifties. When she laughed, she displayed wrinkles on her cheeks, which Rajat took for dimples. Rajat's position was like the defeated King Porus who was brought before the Alexander the Great after the war.

"*Ek Ladki ko dekha….*" When Rajat listens to this song now, he becomes sad and depressed. He walks down the nostalgic memory lanes. Once upon a time, he ruled over a vast empire of butterflies. But now…

A Dog in Manger

Shanker was not a magician in the real sense. He was a popular entertainer — a performer and a conjurer indeed. He took up this job of showing tricks to public by compulsion.

For years, he remained under-employed. He did so many petty jobs but and could not stick to any one of them permanently.

Right from his childhood, he had a natural flair for acting. Right from the school level, he took part in plays. At college level and in inter-university youth festivals, he bagged prizes and medals. He always dreamt of becoming an actor.

The financial position of his family was not sound. His father was a paralytic. Shanker always saw him on the bed. Shanker's mother took up the job of teacher in a private school. She somehow managed her house. Shanker's sisters did well in studies. They got good jobs and were well settled.

Shanker's bend of mind was a bit artistic. He had no interest in studies. He saw no charm in a boring nine to five job at a desk. He was a dreamer, an emotionally charged young man wishing to take the world by storm through the spell of his superb acting.

He had talent but didn't know the right direction that he should take. The small town boys live in a world of daydreaming. They don't know that film industry doesn't hunt in every house for talent. The persons who knock the doors of film studios, struggle to get appointments with producers and directors, sometimes go through even if they are mediocre or average artists. Maybe one is talented but that trait has to be shown to the needy person who may carve out the best in the person.

After doing his graduation somehow, Shanker did petty jobs here and there. He joined a theatre group. These persons were amateur artists who gave one or two performances in a year. They were a friendly group of office goers, petty shopkeepers and amateur students.

The problem with Shanker was that he had over-estimated himself. No doubt, he had good potentials and prospects but he didn't try to reach out where a godfather could patronise him or an agency that could groom him and present him well before a filmmaker. He remained in local circles, performing in small towns in some insignificant theatres. No newspaper focused any story on his talent.

At the age of twenty-five, after trying hard at small jobs, he was strongly motivated by his peer group to go to Delhi. They urged him to try to get a way into National School of Drama or join national level groups, which perform at Kamani Auditorium or Shri Ram Centre, so that someone might notice the hidden talent in him and give him a break.

Now Delhi is a big ocean where people from all across the country come to try their luck. Shanker went from pillar to post.

He found an entry in big projects, but got very small roles. In these roles as a junior artist, he could not bring out the best in himself.

To stay at Delhi, Shanker was forced to do petty part time jobs. Since his educational profile was not impressive enough to enable him to get a good job, the hard jobs he got, left little time for him to devote to theatrical preparation and demands of amateur performances.

By the age of thirty, Shanker had tired himself. His dreams had begun to die. He had lost all hopes of making a dent into what he had been dreaming all through his life. He resigned to his fate and thought of doing something pragmatic and tangibly paying, so that he could have a steady income. His passion for theatre was the main hindrance in getting a good job. He wanted to decide upon one thing — whether to risk his life for theatre, or leave all this and go for a job and get married.

He listened to his heart. He had his peer group — persons who had met with the same fate as he. He thought organising such people to do street plays, which imbibed entertainment with moral preaching. He had some good scripts to work on. He focused on burning issues like decreasing male-female ratio, rape, dowry, corruption, reservation etc.

In the beginning, they got some sponsors too but with increasing serials on various TV channels and decreasing spectators in the public places, these street plays lost their charm and the turnout became poorer and poorer.

And then Shanker took to this job of a performer-cum-entertainer. Now he worked for a living only. He would arrange his performance around lunchtime in front of big office buildings and secretariat. There the officials would have a hearty entertainment and at the end of the show, they would give him some money. He had two young boys whom he called *jamuras* (jokers) on whom he performed witty tricks, amusing magic acts and funny items of jugglery.

He entertained people through humorous titbits, satirical commentary on diabolic leaders, corrupt officials, clever advocates and dishonest businessmen. He had written scores of comic parodies, and through these catchy punches and humorous songs, he would keep the spectators spellbound. This way, they would pass their lunchtime in a humorous way and Shanker would get some earning also.

Soon the public lost interest in these items too. Shanker kept changing places for his shows but now he had to labour hard to amuse the spectators in order to take away a few rupees from their pockets.

That day, it was the limit. Shanker and his boys tried hard on that perspiring and hot summer afternoon.

Shanker pulled hard the ears of his *jamuras*, showed them disappeared, stabbed knives in their stomachs and did all other routine tricks.

The crowd was really very dry and insensitive. Not to mention of clapping at his humorous items, no one even laughed. There was no effect on those stonehearted and numb people.

Shanker and his boys gave up and thought of winding up the show. He showed one last trick and appealed to the public to give them some money.

He gave his long magician's hat to one of his boys and asked him to go round the gathered crowd and collect the contributions from them.

Usually at this point, the crowd starts moving away but still some good people do give him some coins and that was why he was still carrying on the shows.

The boy walked humbly in the crowd with the hat. Many spectators had left the place by now. The boy appealed to everyone present. One by one, they left the scene with indifferent and unmoved look.

Shanker saw his hat empty. He realised the satire that his life had played on him. He laughed at himself and then he raised his head towards the sky. Thanking the Almighty above, he murmured, "Thank you, O Gracious God! From the mob of worthless and evil people, at least my hat came back to me safely."

Picking up

I was in the second year of my degree course. I stayed in a hostel in the city, hundred miles from my village. At the end of every month, I would go to the village. Birju, my childhood friend, would come to know about my visit at once. I would just keep the bag in the house and he would be there before me like a devil. This always annoyed mamma.

She would scold him somewhat affectionately, "The boy has just came. He is tired and you are here to harass him."

Birju was an exception. All other boys of his age went out of the village in the nearby town after matriculating from the high school. They got jobs — some in military service, some in banks and others in private concerns.

Birju remained here. But he had no regrets or guilt. He was unaware of all that. He could not go beyond 8th standard. He was a slow and retarded child. He was fat, sluggish, and out of time.

He wore long loose kurta-pyjama of coarse cotton, made by the local village tailor. He hung round his neck a chequered long scarf, like the one usually adorned by truck drivers on their shoulders.

He usually welcomed me at the bus stop itself. He was there all the day, playing with rowdy village children much younger to his age.

He would greet me with keenness and warm feeling. I would appreciate his emotions. Other people kept him away and ignored him.

When Birju opened his mouth to talk, splinters of dirty saliva gushed out from his mouth. He would show his dirty teeth, uneven and unruly beard, untidy hair and dull moist eyes. He was more than twenty, but his level of apprehension was same as that of a boy of eight. He looked scared, talked in a confused and depressive tone, most of the time lisping many words, though he was good when speaking with his young playmates. But when he talked to adults, he would hesitate and out of fear and sense of inferiority, he would start stammering. Just like a pampered and over-loved child behaves and talks with his over-affectionate mother, Birju behaved childishly.

He could be fooled too easily. Everyone took advantage of his simple, childlike and naïve behaviour. Elder persons, young men and women, and children made fun of him and teased him quite often. He was a butt of ridicule and rustic entertainment. People had framed different funny names for him. Even Birju took delight when they called him by such funny names. He didn't mind at all.

The moment I stepped down from the bus, Birju would surround me. He would start asking from me the same old silly questions he had implored many times before. His expression of eagerness, level of curiosity and surprise would be the same. His facial expressions were natural as if he were asking these things for the first time.

He would ask, "In which class you study?"

I would say, "In B.A. second year."

He would not follow what I would say. He didn't know the names of class beyond 10th. He would make his own calculations and then remark, "Well, I think you are in 13th standard."

I would nod yes.

He would ask the same old question, "Are there class above 16?"

I would say, "Yes Birju, there are classes up to 25."

He would count on his thick dirty ugly fingers and would crack a simple joke, "That means, you will grow old studying all these years. When will you marry then?"

At this point, I would trap him in my net.

I would say, "Birju dear, I am four years younger to you. First of all, you will get married and then my turn will come. I am not like your younger brother who agreed to get engaged before your marriage could be fixed somewhere. I will marry when you have married."

Birju would be caught in a strange fix. He found no ready answer for that. He would be plunged in a strange state of mind — a state of indecision and hesitation. He would look down and would start drawing lines on the earth with his shoes. In his heart, Birju had this fear that it might be true that he would not get married at all.

One day, he met me in the fields. He was coming back from the forest. Seeing me, he showed his readiness to accompany me. In the whole village, Birju loved to talk only to me. I won't offend him and would always listen patiently to what he said. All other persons made fun of him and ridiculed him.

That day, he was carrying a broken V-shaped *chappal* in his hand. After one or two useless talks, we started discussing about the marriage of a young chap of the village. That boy was much younger than Birju.

Unknowingly, I hit his aching bone. I said, "Birju, all the boys of your age are fast getting married. What do your parents say about you? When will they find a girl for you? I am dead sure, they are not serious about this matter. They will leave you single all your life. In your clan, this is a tradition. One or two males always remain single."

Listening to this, Birju was furious and annoyed. His face grew tense, eyes fiery, nostrils swallowed, lips started trembling. From his mouth, angry whistle-like unclear words came gushing.

In a wavering deep and painful voice he said, "Though personally I am not bothered whether I get married or not but the priest of the temple was saying that if a person dies unmarried, his soul rambles aimlessly for years. There is no salvation for him even after death."

When I listened to the clever justification and unnecessary rationalisation of Birju, I could not control my laughter.

I changed the topic, but after a moment, Birju asked, "What is the truth in the advice of the priest?"

But I involved him in another topic.

Birju was dull in studies. His father had a petty provision store in the village. Birju's younger brother did 10th and was recruited as soldier in the army. Birju would have settled somewhere but due the reason that mentally he had not grown and his physical development was also not normal according to his age, he looked a boy of fourteen only even when he had a full-grown beard.

Apart from a small shop, his father also did farming in a small agricultural holding. He was a short-tempered man. He fixed Birju's daily duties for the whole day. In the forenoon, Birju went to the fields to bring green fodder for the cattle and in the afternoon, he did petty errands at the shop.

Birju was not matured enough to devote himself dutifully. He would take three hours to complete a job, which could easily be finished in half an hour. He was very popular with the children of the village. Every boy of ten or eleven was his associate. Most of the time, Birju would attend to petty duties fixed by his father but even then he would forget his work and would start playing with his friends. His father would notice it and would thrash him severely.

Birju was a stubborn boy. He was bent upon becoming the bridegroom's friend in my brother's marriage. Someone had told him that the boy who gets this opportunity gets married immediately. My brother was allergic to Birju and he refused to such a nonsensical proposal. Birju started fasting unto death to press him to fulfil his demand. Only then my brother gave his unwilling approval.

In the marriage, Birju made a good fool of himself. He wore a loose trouser and a tight shirt. Probably that was his brother's attire. The elderly people of the village advised him to remain all the time with the bridegroom escorting him everywhere.

So he did not leave the groom even for a second. Seeing this, the up-to-date and naughty friends of the bride got a good chance of having great fun. They started calling Birju a '*poonch*' (tail), since he would follow the bridegroom all the time. The girls laughed at his childish talks when they found out his mental calibre. These mischievous girls hid Birju's shoes instead of having fun with the bridegroom. Many girls mockingly proposed to marry him.

When Birju's younger brother was married, Birju ran away from his house and remained hidden in field for one whole night in protest. When assured that his marriage would also be arranged within a year, only then he joined the marriage festivities. Later on, he forgot all about that. He was thirty now.

When his father died after a brief illness, he became a bit concerned about domestic affairs. His elder brother was now a retired soldier and held the reins of the house now.

All my close associates were now living out of the village, since we had taken up jobs. We visited village once in six months. My mother would give me the latest development of the events and the whereabouts of people in the village. I enquired about Birju too. Mother told me on my one such visit that Birju was employed as a peon in a private school in a nearby town.

Then next time, I was told that he was married with a mentally retarded girl of a neighbouring village. He took his wife with him. Then I got the news of the birth of his son. I wanted to see him out of curiosity but I was in Delhi and visited my village not on the same days when Birju was in the village.

And finally, we met one day. Birju learned that I had come and he immediately rushed to my house to meet me. We sat in the drawing room.

He was well groomed and looked quite different now. He talked sense and discussed on the topics, like politics, films and scams. I was surprised to listen to him. I thought — is he the same Birju who was so simple in his childhood days? He has become so smart after going away from the village!

He had grown up now. There was a difference of thirty long years between us, but since he was understandable, he asked about my family and I enquired about his. After exchange of all this information, we sat down in silence. My mother, who some thirty years ago wanted that I should not mingle with Birju, was now telling more about him. Watching a matured Birju was a miracle for me.